To my mom. You should have been a chef but you make a damn good nurse.

CONTENTS

OPALS & A NIMBUS OFFICIAL COOKBOOK

NANDER

NOTE FROM THE AUTHOR

Opals & A Nimbus Official Cookbook was a spontaneous project I decided to throw together to pair with my spicy fantasy novel. The idea is that you get a recipe for everything the characters eat in the novel, along with bonus POV and behind-the-scenes information on people and places that inspired aspects of the book.

As it turns out, a cookbook is NOT something you can "throw together." Some recipes were easy because I had them written down on cards and perfected over the years or down to memory. I had gotten many of them over the years and made my own. But other recipes were not so easy.

My paternal grandmother passed away and left behind a pink plastic filing folder full of recipes. I decided to sift through them and use them for the cookbook in her honor. Some were clippings from magazines and ingredient packages. Others were handwritten. She didn't know how to write well, so many of the ingredients didn't make complete sense. I had to guess what some of them said and make the recipes to ensure they weren't awful before publishing.

Some recipes also came from my mother and her deceased relatives. This posed a completely new problem. Some of her older recipes were so weathered and smudged with oils and ingredients that I could hardly read them in some parts. Pair that with her unique cursive, which took a little extra time to decipher. Additionally, my mother sends to eyeball a lot of recipes.

When writing them down from various text messages she's sent over the years, I finally just sat down with her. I would ask, "Hey, mom, how much of *this?*" and she would hold her hands out as if to measure the length of something and say, "About this much." I busted out laughing and said, "Mom, I can't put your hands in the cookbook as a unit of measurement." I remember giving her such a hard time for "eyeballing" it, making jokes for hours. This made it pretty awkward when my editor pointed out that my own recipe for Tuna salad had no measurements, and I caught myself saying, "I just eyeballed it."

I made most of these recipes multiple times to get them right. While I won't claim they are all the best things ever, I am proud to have family recipes, and mine come to life. Also, I want to send a very special thank you to my great Aunt Ella; my grandmother's only living sibling, who helped make sense of some of these recipes and has some phenomenal recipes of her own. I really wish Aunt Ella would write her own cookbook because you guys are really missing out!

<u>The alternate POVs in this book should be read AFTER finishing the book. Spoilers are included.</u>

—DRINKS

BEHIND THE SCENES: MACS ROOFTOP BAR & GRILL

Mac's Rooftop Bar & Grill is inspired by a real place. M Lounge in Orlando, Florida, was an indoor-outdoor bar that I absolutely loved going to. The lower level was a classic car museum, and the outside was an open rooftop overlooking Orlando City proper.

In Chapter 1, Daphne and O'doherty are enjoying dinner and listening to an electric violist. The ambiance in this scene is primarily inspired by my experiences going there with friends. In this photo is me (left) and my best friend Raquel (right) the last time we ever went to M Lounge. Unfortunately, they are permanently closed after the pandemic but will be forever honored in Opals & a Nimbus.

Citrus Creamsicle

CITRUS CREAMSICLE
BONUS RECIPE: MINDY THE BARTENDERS FAVORITE

Ingredients

2 oz Pinnacle Whipped Vodka

4 oz Pulp-free Orange Juice

splash Grenadine (optional)

Whipped Cream

Orange zest

Instructions

Add Vodka, orange juice, and Grenadine to a glass over ice.

Stir gently with a spoon.

Zest orange peel.

Garnish with whipped cream, sprinkling orange zest on top.

C**OO**L BREEZE MOSCOW MULE

FROM CHAPTER 1: DAPHNE- IT'S A FULL MOON

Ingredients:

1 ½ oz Ketel One Cucumber Mint Vodka

3 oz Fever Tree Ginger Beer

¼ lime or 1 lime wedge

2 mint leaves

Ice

Instructions

- In a copper mug, pour vodka over ice.
- Tilt the mug slightly and slowly pour the Ginger Beer in, running it down the side of the cup to avoid too much fizz or splashing.
- Run a lime wedge around the rim of the mug, then squeeze it gently into the drink.
- Drop the lime wedge and mint sprigs into the drink as a garnish.

MIAMI RUM & TONIC
FROM CHAPTER 28: DAPHNE- MY BROKEN WINDOW

Ingredients

2 oz Siesta Key Coconut Rum

2 oz Tonic

1 Lime wedge

1 Block Ice

Instructions

- Pour rum over Ice.

- Add tonic.

- Rum lime wedge on the rim and garnish with lime.

BEHIND THE SCENES: OUR WEDDING DRINK

After my husband proposed, we did what most couples do: go venue shopping. We stopped by the Ritz Carlton in Sarasota, Florida, and decided to have lunch there to sample the bar. Their Rum & Tonic was one of the best I ever had. The secret was the locally sourced rum, Siesta Key Coconut Rum. With a little squeeze of lime, it was both refreshing and low-calorie. This photo was taken in 2019.

Unfortunately, I worked as an ICU nurse when the COVID pandemic hit, which meant our wedding was canceled. Instead, we married on the beach with just our parents, officiant (his aunt), and photographer. It was perfectly intimate and low-stress, and I wouldn't change it for the world.

SUNSET MIMOSA

FROM CHAPTER 4: DAPHNE- THE CLOUD WAITED

Ingredients

1/3 chilled Organic orange juice with high pulp

1/3 cup chilled Champagne or sparkling wine

Instructions

- Pour champagne or sparkling wine into the glass.

- Top off with orange juice.

BEHIND THE SCENES: CHEERS TO THE ILLUSTRATOR, DEXTOR ISAAC

I would be remiss not to mention the stunning artistry in Opals & a Nimbus. I knew I wanted the book to be illustrated, but never in a million years did I think I would partner with one of my favorite artists to illustrate my debut novel. I found Dexter Isaacs's page on Instagram and was instantly in love with his skills. His work with lighting and color is unmatched and stunning. Working with him has been an absolute pleasure. He seems to just *get it.* For every scene I gave him, he worked up a better piece than I could have imagined. It is very hard for me to pick which of the illustrations he did for this book is my favorite, but this one of Pol from Chapter 11 is pretty high up there. Some of the photos I gave him to work with were from the airplane window as my husband and I took off for our honeymoon from Miami airport. The shadow you see on the water is drawn from that. It made this one of the most special pieces to me and I teared up a little when I saw it.

ARIAL NEGRONI
FROM CHAPTER 1: DAPHNE- IT'S A FULL MOON

Ingredients

1 oz Aviator Gin

1 oz Campari

1 oz Sweet Red Vermouth

½ cup of ice

1 fresh Organic Orange, Washed

Materials

Shaker

Matches

Instructions:

- Add ice to a shaker. Pour in equal parts gin, Campari, and Sweet Red Vermouth.
- Cover and shake.
- Strain the contents, pouring only the liquid into a glass.
- Cut a round from the orange rind. Light a match and hold it a few inches from the top of the drink. Hold the rind, orange side down, over the match about 3 inches or so over the match. If there's soot on the peel it is too close.
- Let the match heat the surface of the orange peel for a few seconds to warm the oil within the rind. Quickly squeeze the rind hard to release the oil onto the surface of the drink. NOTE: The flame will grow for a moment when you do this. Take care not to burn yourself.
- Rub the peel around the rim of the glass and drop it in the drink to garnish.

SPEIR COFFEE

FROM CHAPTER 40: O'DOHERTY- IF I SURVIVE HIM

Ingredients

Glass mug

6oz Strong hot coffee (recommend Peet's Major Dickenson's Blend)

2 oz Kahlua

1 oz Old Bushmills Irish whisky

Whip cream to taste

Drizzle Creme de Menthe (optional)

Instructions

- Pour the coffee into a glass mug.
- Add Kahlua and whisky.
- Stir.
- Top with whipped cream.
- Drizzle whipped cream with Creme De Menthe if desired.

BONUS SCENE
POL- CHAPTERS 4 - 6

I found her. After years of feeling the pull to the urine and tobacco-scented city of Miami, where too many humans dwell, I found my lost mate. Daphne was the one prophecies spoke of.

She had been running from the same unnatural storm that I tracked to the back of the woods. Our enemies from Cumbre found a way to dissolve the barriers that keep outsiders from manipulating the weather in our territory. A stormmaker formed the tornado and left it to ravage the area that she happened to be in. On this night, I was ready to take the twister down, under cover of trees where no mortal human could see me, when someone tugged on my arm. Startled, and assuming that the storm's maker had engaged in combat, I threw her to the ground without a second thought. But when I saw her lying in the wet heap of pine needles, hair spiraling up into the storm's violent wind, blood smeared across her face, something clicked. The pull was unmistakable. The attraction to her was intense and primitive. If a storm weren't about to kill us both, I would have pulled her onto my nimbus cloud and flown her to safety. I would have claimed her before we even reached the Sky Realm.

But something wasn't right. She only reacted with shock and terror. It was as if the pull I felt had no one pulling back. Ouran, King of Cumbre, hindered her magic; her eyes had no gemstone for irises. Her skin had no aura mist to protect her from the abrasive air in this realm. She seemed utterly human.

There was no time to question her about the discrepancies. I had to dissolve the storm and track its maker. I yelled for her to take cover and formed a nimbus cloud. Before jumping onto it, I yelled for her again, but the approaching twister veiled my orders. Mounting my cloud, I saw her finally scrambling away in my periphery. I moved my cloud up and toward the storm and fought it harder than I ever had before.

Rage and adrenaline coursed through me. Cumbre may have rendered my mate human, but they would not take her life from me in this storm. I managed to dissolve the tornado quickly. I pushed out my magic far and laid a layer of cold air within a mile of the site to prevent more storms from forming so quickly.

When I looked down from my nimbus cloud, I saw her unconscious, bloodied, and too close to the canal's water line. I rushed to her, lowering my cloud fast, and scooped her in my arms. She was like ice, her lips blue, her skin pale except for the scrapes and cuts all over her. Her hair hung heavy with water.

"Hey! Wake up." I shook her, and she barely roused but for a groan and shiver trembling over her lip. A fast wind rustled the tree-tops nearby—*the storm maker.*

I had to hide her and find this enemy before they hurt her or did any more damage. I'd capture them and take them to Loanan for interrogation, but only after securing her. I quickly carried her onto my nimbus cloud and hid her body in the nearby irrigation drain of the canal. She would be in significant pain, so I left a gift on her wrist. Using fallen trees, I dammed the canal on either side of the large pipe and encased it in ice. Then, I formed a stairway into the steep canal's side for her, should she need a quick escape. I cast a protective enchantment over the space so no one would see the dams.

Another rustling of leaves startled me. It was one of my men waiting for orders on his small cumulus cloud. Quietly, I signaled for them to track the maker north. When they zipped off, I gathered Daphne's belongings and dropped them under a broken tree. Before I left to aid my men in the hunt, I memorized every detail of her human ID. *Daphne.*

And that is how I found myself here in her house as she showered in the darkness of 03:00. The water was running in the master bath when I misted to the hall near her kitchen. The house was dark; the power was out. With a limp from the fight, I stepped across the foyer, crossing into the shadows of her kitchen. I studied the space, running my hand over every surface as I passed. I stopped in front of the sink, noticing a small medication bottle on the counter. When I popped the lid open, I recoiled at the stench. *Poison.*

There was no doubt in my mind; This is why she was presenting as a human. I capped the bottle and pocketed it. I'd bring it back to Uripe and have him figure out what in the Regnum Magma it was and how to get it out of her system. I opened some cabinets until I found a glass. Walking toward the sound of running water, I hovered my hand over the cup and used my magic to fill it with water.

Her bed sheets were soft as I bunched them in my fist and pressed them to my face. I could smell someone else on them and snarled internally. My eyes found the bathroom door, which she must have left wide open to let in any light from the moon outside. The glass clinked against the nightstand. The shower turned off, and I looked over my shoulder. I pulled the strings loose from a leather pouch, reached in, and pinched the grainy dust. I sprinkled it into the water and stirred it with my finger. Before pulling it out, I formed a round ball of ice at my fingertip. It bobbed as I withdrew my finger. Wiping the liquid on my pants, I watched her in the doorway and listened to her toweling herself dry, wincing a little as she traced the cloth over sore spots and fresh wounds.

She would come out any moment. I supposed I should give her some privacy. I misted outside of her window and leaned against the wall. I would ensure she had her water before I left to report that Daphne, the lost Princess of Valare, had been found. I had to report back soon and didn't have time to explain, but then she did something that made me stay a little longer.

MIAMI COFFEE
FROM CHAPTER 6 DAPHNE: BUT I WAS FLOATING

Ingredients

1-2 tbsp Cafe Bustelo, depending on the desired strength

1 cup whole milk

2 oz Disaronno velvet cream liqueur (optional) OR Rum Chada peppermint bark

2 tbsp Agave (optional)

Instructions

- Put milk in a microwave-safe mug. Heat for 1-1 ½ minutes.

- Froth milk with frother for 30-45 seconds.

- Stir in Cafe Bustelo until foam and liquid are tinted brown.

- Add liquor of choice and stir.

- Sweeten with additional agave to taste.

BEHIND THE SCENES: WHEN DAPHNE FLOATS

In chapter 6, Daphne is floating above her bed in an almost hypnotic, altered state. This isn't the only time Daphne finds herself floating. In chapter 19, she realizes Pol has lifted them on a cloud as they dance. Some of my favorite childhood media inspire both of these scenes. Floating above the bed was an homage to Sabrina The Teenage Witch. Played by Melissa Joan Hart, Sabrina is seen floating over her bed on her 16th birthday as a sign that her witchy powers have manifested. As a young girl, I even had a Sabrina Barbie with a bed that would levitate the doll. The floating dance was inspired by Casper (the friendly ghost). I remember as a young girl swooning over real-life Casper dancing with Christina Ricci at their dance and making them float. They weren't floating on a cloud, but this isn't a story about Casper; It's about magical beings who live amongst us and rise on clouds.

CALM FROM THE SOIL TEA

FROM CHAPTER 20 O'DOHERTY: THE GHOST SHE SAW BESIDE ME

Ingredients

⅓ tbsp dried chamomile buds

1 ⅔ tbsp dried spearmint leaves

⅓ tbsp rose hips

1 ¾ tbsp almond milk

Sugar or agave to taste

Instructions

- Place the dried herbs in the mortar and crush with the pestle until ground to the preferred consistency.
- Place herbs into a steeper. Place the steeper in the mug or tea cup. Pour boiling water over it. Allow to steep for 3-5 minutes.
- Remove the steeper.
- Add in Almond milk to taste.
- Sweeten with honey or sugar to taste.

GINGER TUMMY TEA
CHAPTER 30 O'DOHERTY: OH. MY. GOD.

Ingredients

1-2" Ginger root

1 tbsp + agave

4 cups water

Instructions

- Bring water to a boil in a pot.

- Meanwhile, peel and finely dice ginger root.

- Add ginger to boiling water and lower heat to a simmer. Let simmer for 5-10 minutes or until the water is an amber brown.

- Pour into a mug and sweeten with agave to taste.

BEHIND THE SCENES: JESULA

Jesula is introduced in this scene and is possibly one of the most underrated characters of the series. She is inspired by several real-life union leaders, including those from Phoenix, Arizona, Kissimmee, Florida, and Orlando, Florida. Their bravery and no-nonsense confidence made Jesula the character you will grow close to throughout the series.

I knew Jesula would mean more to me than I could initially give her credit for, so I plan to focus heavily on her backstory in subsequent books in the Nimbus series. As Jesula is a Haitian immigrant, I really had to dive deep into Haiti's history. The things I learned in the first four days of researching Haiti's fascinating history will propel the plot in what I expect to be book three.

—SNACKS & APPS

- Creamy Cucumber Bites
- Calzone Bites
- Apricot Baked Pastries
- Cranberry Bites

CREAMY CUCUMBER BITES
FROM CHAPTER 9 O'DOHERTY: A CHILLED EMPTINESS

Ingredients

3-4 long cucumbers

4 oz cream cheese (softened)

4 oz sour cream

2 large garlic cloves or 3 small (minced)

3 tbsp ranch seasoning

½ cup shredded cheese

1 tbsp chopped chives

½ cup bacon crumbles or 6-10 thin strips of bacon (crumbled)

2 tbsp dill weed

¾ tbsp dried minced onion

½-1 tsp celery salt (to taste)

Instructions

- Wash produce. Peel cucumbers in a striped pattern, then cut them into 1" pieces. With a small spoon, scoop out some of the cucumber pulp from the center of one side to form little cups.
- If not using premade bacon crumbles, cook bacon to a crisp and crumble.
- Combine the remaining ingredients in a bowl (Cream cheese, Sour Cream, cheese, garlic, chives, ranch seasoning salt, dill weed, and minced onion).
- Spoon the mixture into the cucumber cups and top with OR put the mixture in a ziplock bag, cut the corner, and pipe the mixture into the cucumber cups.
- Top with crumbled bacon.

CALZONE BITES

FROM CHAPTER 39 O'DOHERTY: ASH IN MY HANDS

Ingredients

2 tubes of Pillsbury pizza crust dough sheets OR see Pizza dough recipe

2 cups Ricotta cheese

2 cups Pizza sauce (premade or see pizza sauce recipe)

Small slices of Pepperoni (or other topping)

8oz package of BelGioioso Mozzarella Pearls

1 tsp Garlic minced

2-3 basil leaves, sliced

Olive oil

Garlic salt

Crisco

You will need an empanada press and circular cookie cutter (this recipe used a 3.7-inch Empanada press with a 3.9-inch cookie cutter. Ingredients per calzone may vary depending on the size of your press.

Instructions

- If using the pizza dough recipe, take out the dough and let it sit out for 30 minutes to 1 hour before using. Preheat the oven to 350 degrees.

- Crease a baking sheet with Crisco.

- Roll out pizza dough. Cut out circles large enough to fit in an empanada press using a circle cookie cutter. Then, lay dough circles in the empanada press.

- Spoon 1-1 1/2 tsp of pizza sauce in the center of the dough and use the bottom of the measuring spoon to spread it out.

- Spoon in 1 tbsp Ricotta cheese in the center, using the bottom of the measuring spoon to press it down and spread it.

- Add a pinch of minced garlic and a strip of basil into the center.
- Add 1-2 small pepperonis or other desired filling into the center of the calzone.
- Add 2-3 (depending on how full the center already is) mozzarella pearls into the center along the seam of the empanada press.
- Press the empanada maker shut, sealing the dough. Place the mini calzone onto the greased baking sheet. Repeat until you run out of dough.
- Brush with olive oil and sprinkle with garlic salt sparingly.
- Bake for 15-20 minutes or until golden brown.
- Let cool for 3-5 minutes and enjoy.

APRICOT BAKED PASTRIES
FROM CHAPTER 19 DAPHNE: CLOSE TO TOUCHING

Ingredients

2 tubes of Pillsbury Croissant Dough sheets or see the Croissant recipe

¾ cups apricot preserves divided)

½ pound sliced deli honey ham cut sandwich thick

1 round 8 oz Brie cheese, rind removed

1 egg

Crisco

Everything Bagel seasoning to taste

You will need an Empanada press and a round cookie cutter. Croissant dough shrinks slightly when cut. For this recipe, I used a 2.5-inch empanada press with a 3.8-inch cookie cutter. The ingredients for the filling may vary depending on the size of your empanada press.

Instructions

- If using the croissant recipe, take the dough out to rest for 30 minutes. Preheat the oven to 360 degrees—pre-grease the baking sheet with Crisco.

- Peel the rind off the brie and cut the brie into 1 ½-inch cubes—slice ham into 1 1/2-inch thick strips.

- Roll out croissant dough. Use a round cookie cutter to cut a circle out. Lay the circle inside the empanada press. If it isn't large enough to fit at the edges, roll it out more, but ensure the dough does not become too thin.

- Spoon 1 tbsp of apricot preserves into the center. Then, lay a strip of ham on top, folding it into itself to fit in the center. Add 1 cube of brie cheese in the center, pressing to flatten if the center is too full. Press the pastry shut with the empanada press.

- Place the pastry on a greased baking pan. Repeat until you run out of dough.
- Beat one egg in a bowl with a whisk until just blended. Brush the pastries with egg mixture. Sprinkle everything bagel seasoning on top. Use sparingly, as this can make them too salty.
- Bake at 350 degrees for 12-17 minutes or until golden brown.
- Let cool for 3-5 minutes. Best served warm.

CRANBERRY BITES
FROM CHAPTER 14 O'DOHERTY: MY SAFE PLACE

Ingredients

1 Pillsbury Croissant dough sheet OR see Croissant recipe

8-ounce Brie cheese round (rind removed)

1 cup whole berry cranberry sauce

½ cup pistachios (finely chopped)

Fresh whole rosemary sprigs

Flour

Cooking spray

Instructions

- If not a nonstick mini muffin tin, spray the mini muffin tin with cooking spray OR line the tin with mini liners.
- Place the croissant dough sheets on a lightly greased cutting board.
- Cut the crescent dough into 24 squares, about 2 ½ inches.
- Cut Brie cheese into 24 small equal pieces. Roll into grape-size balls.
- Press dough squares into the muffin tin slots to make cups.
- Place one brie ball into each dough cup.
- Spoon enough cranberry sauce over Brie balls to cover them but not overflow.
- Pluck younger growths of rosemary from the stem.
- Top with crushed pistachios and a sprig of rosemary.
- Bake for 15 minutes or until the crescent pastry is a light golden brown.
- Place the bites on a serving plate and serve warm.

—BREADS & NOODLES

- BONUS SCENE
- Bagels
- BEHIND THE SCENES: Grandmas Bagel Recipe
- Pizza Crust
- Manicotti Noodles
- Croissants Two Ways
- Flakey Biscuits
- Artison Loaf
- EXCERPT FROM CHAPTER 4 Daphne: The Cloud Waited for Him with bonus commentary from author

BONUS SCENE
POL- CHAPTERS 13-15

Waking up in a new place for the first time is always disorienting. I pulled myself from Daphne's guest bed and wrapped the sheet around my waist. My clothes were still warm from the dryer when I pulled them on, taking care not to make too much noise and wake Daphne. She had made homemade bagels and left them out for me. I cut one down the center, held a palm over it, and released heat to toast it.

I walked into her room quietly. She was sleeping deeply. The gray glow of predawn bled through the window and I made my way to her bedside. I grazed a finger down her chin. She didn't budge. I unclasped the necklace from my neck and worked it around hers with magic. My muscles stiffened in its absence, but I would be fine. I knelt down to clasp it together by hand and pulled the geode pendant down her chest. Her skin was warm under my hand, and comfort grew inside me. She was coming home with me soon. *She is mine.*

Her fat dog trotted in and jumped on the bed, resting her jowls on Daphne's leg and looking at me curiously. Daphne didn't move. I assumed she would want to bring the pup with her to Loanan. It wouldn't be out of the question. We had our version of dogs there, but they were much hairier and had wings and long bodies. Their paws were usually much larger in proportion than a Regnum Solo dog would be. They could also squeeze into tight places, much like a cat, and had long mains that ran down their spine to their tails. Other than those things, this Polpetta dog should fit in fine.

I stayed only a moment more to admire my mate's face. It was pressed into the pillow and leaking drool, but she was still as beautiful as ever. I covered her shoulder with the duvet and closed the door behind me while leaving her room.

I took a bite as I mounted my nimbus cloud. It was the freshest bagel I had ever eaten. I tried to peek through her window before raising it to the sky. And then, I left to prepare for her arrival. Everything from the garden to her room would be perfect for her; purple hyacinths and clothes to make her feel welcome.

Finally.

Meet the bagel.

Fleischmann's® Yeast would like to introduce you to homemade bagels.

What's a bagel? It's a roll with a crusty outside, chewy inside, and an unmistakable hole in the center. Now Fleischmann's® Yeast has a recipe for delicious bagels you can bake yourself. Try the original recipe, or variations, including caraway, poppy seed, sesame, onion, and many more.

BAGELS: Makes 1 dozen

4½ to 5 cups unsifted flour
3 tablespoons sugar
1 tablespoon salt
2 pkgs. Fleischmann's

Water
2 tablespoons Fleischmann's® Margarine
1 tablespoon

BAGELS

FROM CHAPTER 15: DAPHNE: JUST ABOVE THE CLOUD LINE

Ingredients

4 ½ to 5 cups unsifted flour

3 tbsp white granulated sugar

1 tbsp salt

2 packets of activated dry yeast (<u>Fleischmann's</u>)

Water

2 tbsp margarine or unsalted Kerrygold butter

1 tbsp white granulated sugar

2 tsp salt

1 egg white

Instructions

- Mix 1 ½ cups flour, 3 tbsp sugar, and 1 tbsp salt and yeast.

- Heat 1 ½ cups water and margarine to 120 degrees. Add to dry ingredients and beat for 2 minutes at medium speed with an electric mixer.

- Add ½ cup flour and beat at high speed for two minutes.

- Stir in more flour (½ a cup at a time, up to 4.5 cups in total) to make a stiff dough. Stop using the mixer after about 3 cups and change to kneading.

- On a floured board, knead for 8-10 minutes. Set in a greased bow, turn to grease top. Cover; let rise in a warm draft-free area for 1 hour.

- Punch down dough. Cover; let rest for 15 minutes.

- Preheat the oven to 375 degrees.

- In a large skillet, heat 1-inch of water over medium-low heat to a simmer and add the remaining salt and sugar.

- Divide dough into 12 pieces and shape into smooth balls. With a floured finger, poke a 1-inch hole in each.
- 3 at a time, drop bagels into simmering water. Cook for 3 minutes, turn and cook for 2 minutes, turn again, cook for 1 more minute, then drain on a towel. You may need to replenish salted and sugared water between batches.
- Place on a greased baking sheet.
- Mix the egg whites with 1 tbsp water and mix lightly with a fork. Brush the egg wash over the top of the bagel. Season the bagel as desired (salt, sesame, caraway, poppy, or everything bagel seasoning).
- Bake at 375 degrees for 20-25 min. Remove from the sheet and cool on a wire rack.

BEHIND THE SCENES: GRANDMAS BAGEL RECIPE

When my Italian grandmother died, she left behind a pink plastic filing folder filled with recipes. My Aunt Theresa asked if I wanted them, and I was thrilled to have them, hoping I would come across her famous spaghetti sauce recipe that she took to the grave. Some recipes were handwritten, which was challenging because she didn't know how to write well. Others were clippings from magazines that she had collected over the years. I pulled many of the recipes in this book from that collection. The recipe for Bagels featured in this cookbook is primarily inspired by a magazine clipping dated 1981! It appears to have been an ad for Fleischmann's Yeast titled "Meet The Bagel." In this advertisement, they go on to explain what a bagel is! Reading this, I couldn't help but laugh at the idea of learning what something as common as a bagel was. The clipping was perfectly preserved, not a wrinkle or oil stain. That is, until I made the bagels to test the recipe. After a small splash of some ingredients got on it, I typed up the recipe and tucked it away. After making the recipe, I decided it needed a little tweaking, but I loved the fresh taste so much that I had to feature it in the novel and this, the tandem cookbook.

PIZZA CRUST
FROM CHAPTER 4 DAPHNE: THE CLOUD WAITED FOR HIM

PAIRS WITH MARGARITA PIZZA RECIPE

Ingredients

1 ½ cups warm water (100-110 degrees)

2 tsp white granulated sugar

2 packets (or ¼ oz each) of active dry yeast

4 cups all-purpose flour sifted and leveled.

1 tsp salt

¼ cup extra virgin olive oil

Instructions

- Pour water into a large metal or glass bowl. Ensure it is between 100 and 110 degrees. Add yeast and sugar. Let it stand until foamy, about 6 minutes. When done, add olive oil, reserving about ½ tbsp for later.

- In a separate bowl, mix flour and salt. Make a well. Mix wet ingredients into dry ingredients. Mix until a sticky dough forms.

- Use olive oil to grease the original metal or glass bowl; you don't have to clean it first. Turn the dough into the glass bowl and rotate to coat it with olive oil. Brush the top with olive oil. Cover with plastic wrap and set aside in a warm, draft-free place until the dough doubles in size (approximately 1 hour).

- Turn dough onto a lightly floured surface and gently knead 5-6 times, forming it into a ball. Let the dough rise again for about 10 more minutes.

- If not used immediately, place in a gallon ziplock bag and refrigerate. Take it out to rest at room temperature 30 minutes to 1 hour prior to using it.

MANICOTTI NOODLES

FROM CHAPTER 14 O'DOHERTY: MY SAFE PLACE

PAIRS WITH MANICOTTI RECIPE

Ingredients

3 cups all-purpose flour

3/4 tsp salt

2 organic eggs

Warm water as needed

Instructions

- I recommend the kitchen aid mixer with the spaghetti attachment.

- Sift flour and salt together, working out lumps.

- Make a well in the middle, using the bottom of a 1-cup dry measuring cup.

- Crack eggs and drop them into the well. Gradually blend within with a fork and slowly add enough warm water to form a stiff dough.

- Knead until smooth. Transfer to a bowl, cover, and let it stand for 15 minutes.

- Cut in half and roll the two dough onto a floured surface into two thin sheets.

- Cut into rectangles 4x5 inches. Let dry for 1 hour.

- Boil 5 cups of salted water. Cook the rectangles for 10 minutes in rapidly boiling salted water. Drain, rinse in cold water, and drain again.

- Use immediately (see Manicotti recipe).

CROISSANTS TWO WAYS (COCONUT-CRUSTED CROISSANTS)

FROM CHAPTER 32 DAPHNE: THAT ROCK!

PAIRS WITH CARIBBEAN JERK PULLED PORK RECIPE OR APRICOT PASTRY RECIPE

Ingredients

4 cups flour

⅓ cup sugar

4 tsp active dry yeast

2 ¼ tsp pink Himalayan salt

¼ cups unsalted butter (cold)

1 cup milk (cold)

1 large egg beaten with 1 tsp water or milk

Shredded raw coconut (if making coconut-crusted croissants)

Instructions

- Combine flour, sugar, yeast, and salt in a large bowl and whisk them together until combined.
- Slice butter into ⅛-inch thick slices and toss in the flour mixture to coat.
- Add milk and mix together until a stiff dough forms.
- Wrap the dough tightly in plastic wrap and chill it in the fridge for about 1 hour.
- Roll the dough out on a lightly floured surface into a long rectangular shape.

- Fold it into thirds (like a letter), turn 90 degrees, and repeat 3-5 more times, or until the dough has large streaks of butter in it but is smooth and flat. The butter should still be stiff; chill the dough if it becomes soft.
- Wrap tightly again and chill for one more hour. Divide the dough in half and roll each portion to a thickness of about ⅛-inch in a long rectangle shape about 10 inches by 20 inches long. (If making apricot-baked pastry, continue your process using that recipe.)
- Cut the dough into long pizza-shaped triangles about 5 inches wide at the end. Roll it from wide to thin end, tucking the point underneath at the end.
- Place on a parchment-lined baking sheet, cover loosely with plastic wrap, and allow to double in for about (1 1/2 hours).
- Preheat the oven to 375 degrees. Beat one egg in a small bowl until mixed thoroughly. Brush the top of the croissant with the egg mixture. (If making coconut-crusted croissants as a side for jerked pulled pork and arugula salad, press shredded coconut to a wet surface to gently stick.)
- Bake for 15-20 minutes or until puffed and golden.

FLAKEY BISCUITS

FROM CHAPTER 10 O'DOHERTY: THE SEASON OF GIFTING

PAIRS EGGS BENNY RECIPE

Ingredients:

1 ¾ cups all-purpose flour

2 ½ tsp baking powder

1 tsp freshly ground pink Himalayan salt OR sea salt

6 tbsp chilled unsalted Kerrygold butter (cut into small pieces)

¾ cup whole milk OR almond milk

Instructions

- Preheat the oven to 450 degrees. Grease a baking sheet with Crisco or butter OR line the baking sheet with parchment paper.
- Whisk together the flour, baking powder, and salt in a medium bowl, working out any lumps. Using a fork, combine the butter and flour mixture until it is crumbly. Slowly stir in milk, mixing with the fork.
- FOR SOFTER BISCUITS: Transfer dough to the baking sheet 2 tablespoons at a time. Place on the lined baking sheet.
- FOR FIRMER BISCUITS: Knead the dough and roll it out ¾ inches thick. Then, use a round cookie or biscuit cutter or the rim of a round glass to cut about 12 biscuits. (Reroll any scraps and cuts.)
- Bake the biscuits for 13 to 15 minutes (add 3 to 4 additional minutes if you've frozen the dough) until golden brown. Cool slightly and serve warm.

ARTISAN LOAF
FROM CHAPTER 19 DAPHNE: CLOSE TO TOUCHING

Ingredients

1 ½ tsp activated dry yeast

1 ¾ cups of water (100-110 degrees)

3 ½ cups plus 1 tbsp all-purpose flour (divided)

2 tsp salt

1 tbsp cornmeal or additional flour

Instructions

- In a large bowl, dissolve yeast in water. If the yeast packet calls for sugar, skip that step. The water should be between 100 and 110 degrees, as yeast is a living organism.

- In another large bowl, mix 3 ½ cups flour and salt, sifting out lumps. Create a well in the center of the flour using the bottom of a 1-cup dry measuring cup.

- Using a rubber spatula, add the yeast mixture, stirring just until smooth (the dough will be sticky). Do not knead the dough. Cover the bowl with plastic wrap and let it rise at room temperature for about 1 hour in a warm, draft-free area.

- Punch down the dough. Turn it onto a lightly floured surface. Pat it into a 9-inch square, then fold it into thirds. You should be forming a 9x3-inch rectangle. Fold the rectangle into thirds again in the other direction, forming a 3-inch square. Turn the dough over into a bowl greased with olive oil or Crisco.

- Cover the bowl with plastic wrap or cling wrap and let it rise at room temperature until almost doubled, about 1 hour, in a warm draft-free area.

- Punch down the dough again and repeat the folding process. Return the dough to the same bowl and refrigerate overnight, covered.
- Line the bottom of a disposable foil roasting pan with parchment paper. Dust the paper sparingly with flour and then liberally with cornmeal. Turn the dough onto a floured surface. Knead gently 8 times. Shape the dough into a 6-inch round loaf. Then, place the load into the prepared pan. Dust the top of the loaf with the remaining 1 tbsp flour and about 1 tsp of cornmeal. Cover the pan with plastic wrap and let it rise at room temperature until the dough expands in size to 7 ½ -in the loaf, about 1 1/4 hours.
- Preheat the oven to 500 degrees. Using a sharp knife, make a slash (¼ in deep) across the top of the loaf. Cover the pan tightly with regular foil. Bake on the lowest oven rack for 25 minutes.
- Reduce the oven setting to 450 degrees. Remove the foil and bake for an additional 25-30 minutes longer or until deep golden brown. Transfer the loaf to a wire rack to cool.

EXCERPT FROM CHAPTER 4 DAPHNE: THE CLOUD WAITED FOR HIM

WITH BONUS COMMENTARY FROM THE AUTHOR

I made it just past the first block before hearing the sound of a freight train. Looking to my right I could see the dark shadow of a funnel cloud. It was forming just a couple blocks away, illuminated by lightning and sparks from power lines. I saw it touch down and head in my direction. Dread filled my gut.

I look toward the restaurant and then back toward my car. They were about the same distance. Neither was likely to do well in a tornado. I backtracked and darted around the corner of the jewelry store. I ran fast down the alley toward a wooded area. There was an irrigation canal behind those woods. I knew it would be the lowest ground I could find. The question was, could I make it there? I had to try.

The sound of my feet crashing against wet pavement shifted to the crunching of leaves. The deeper I ran the darker it was. No light from street lamps or store signs could reach that far back. I struggled to navigate in the darkness. I pulled out my phone to use its light. It only helped me see a few feet ahead. Occasionally, lightning cracked overhead, letting me see a little farther in front of me.

The rain poured relentlessly. The hail grew larger and more frequent. My computer bag shielded my head. Yet I still cringed as hail pelted my body. The train-like sound only got louder. Blood dripping from my brow blurred my vision, tinting it red. With every flash of lightning, the blood gave a dreadful red tinge to the dark woods. The trees behind me groaned as they bent until they were ripped from their roots or snapped at their trunks. I cried out running deeper and faster. Branches and debris stung my skin in the whirling wet wind. Red flashes of tree limbs zipped past my face. My soaked scrubs clung to my frame. Finally, a clearing came into view. The canal was close.

But a branch caught my shin. I toppled over just inches from the canal drop-off. My body hit the wet ground with a hard smack. Then, my bag and purse flew forward. They bounced and tumbled down the steep canal landing at the waterline. The light of my phone behind me caught my attention. I lunged for it, but something else caught my eye. My jaw dropped at the sight.

Under a bolt of lightning that stabbed the sky, the world lit up for a long moment. The roaring twister was closing in just a football field's length away. It was a terrifying machine of nightmares coiling around itself. But just a few yards ahead of me was a man. He just stood there, his hands up. It was like he expected to wrestle the storm.

"Get down!" I screamed. But my voice was lost in the ripping wind. I pushed against the wind to get to him. The strobing lightning guided me. Rain cleaned the blood from my vision just enough to see him better. I would pull his crazy ass down to the safety of the canal. I grabbed his arm and pulled. "Hey!"

The man startled, pushing me down. He raised an open palm and stopped to meet my eyes. Laying at his feet I looked up at him. My eyes squinted against the sting of pine needles and rain. But he stared at me unflinchingly. He looked shocked that I was there. He was thin, tall, and pale. He had dark, medium-length hair. But his eyes were what stunned me. His irises were a shimmering opalescent. It was as if the gem itself were pushed into his damn sockets. Every flash of lightning made them shimmer in pale pastels. His shirtless body was wet. A slow, weightless barrier surrounded his skin a few inches. It was like an aura of mist.

I drew a sharp breath and backed up on my arms, kicking against the ground. My heart pounded at the inhuman site. His mouth moved but I could hear nothing over the chaos. Then he pointed behind me. The rain slapped my face. My wet hair tossed in the wind as I slid farther back. Still unable to pull my eyes from him, I gripped the earth beneath me for grounding. He screamed again into the vacuum. His body then turned toward a gray mass growing in front of him. It was a small storm cloud… Hovering just feet above the ground, the cloud waited for him. He jumped on the cloud, and it lifted him higher and closer to the storm. He lifted his arms again in a strange fighting stance, palms open and forward.

I flipped to my knees. Scrambling to crawl away, I shivered violently. I was hallucinating, and I couldn't waste any more time. I made it to my feet, still crouched and panting. The edge of the canal looked like a rough descent. Gripping a thick root, I started to lower myself into it. Then, my head was hit by something large and hard. The root ripped out of my palm, skinning it raw. My vision strobed as I fell forward. I tumbled down the steep, muddy drop-off and landed at the waterline with a splash. Laying on my back, I groaned and looked to the sky. As my vision faded to dark, I could only see a brief glimpse of the man surfing atop a cloud high above me, using an unseen force to send ripples into the storm.

COMMENTARY FROM THE AUTHOR

This was a fun scene for me to write because it is primarily based on a very morbid poem I wrote when I was about twelve years old. I couldn't remember it if I tried, but I remember the beats and pacing perfectly and the overall theme of the poem, which was essentially—for whatever weird reason—about waking up in an irrigation drain. The poem inspired the tail end of this scene and largely influenced the subsequent scene in Daphne's POV.

People sometimes ask authors, "Are you a pantser (write the story by the seat of your pants) or a plotter (plot the story out and stick to that structure)? But I once heard an author describe her method as being a "quilter," where the author already knows a scene that they want to happen without any context around the scene. They sew it into the story so those scenes will occur as they build the story around them. I think quilting is the best answer in the case of me writing Opals & a Nimbus, not only because of this teen angst phase wax poetic poem working its way into this scene. There are several things I knew I wanted to happen in the book before I had a clear plan for the book.

Another of those quilted things was to pay homage to one of my first favorite cartoons. Yes, Dragon Ball Z was a big inspiration for the type of magical beings in this book. Pol, the man in this scene, is a Goku and Adam Driver mashup!

—SAUCES & DRESSINGS

- Pasta Sauce
- Pizza Sauce
- Pesto Sauce
- Hollandaise Sauce
- Ceasar Dressing

PASTA SAUCE

FROM CHAPTER 14 O'DOHERTY: MY SAFE PLACE

PAIRS WITH MANICOTTI RECIPE

Ingredients

½ lb lean ground beef

½ lb mild Italian sausage

24 oz Contadina Tomato sauce

1 can Rotel (mild) or crushed tomatoes

2 tbsp sugar to taste (to cut acid)

1 tbsp salt

1 tbsp pepper

4 TBSP fresh Oregano finely chopped

4 tbsp garlic powder

2 tbsp Italian seasoning

3 whole bay leaves

Instructions

- Mix meat and sausage in a large bowl until blended.

- In a large sauce pot, cook the meat, breaking it into small crumbles. Drain

- Add tomato sauce, Rotel, salt, pepper, garlic powder, Italian seasoning, and oregano to the saucepan with the meat mixture until blended.

- Heat over low-medium heat until just more than a simmer, stirring frequently.

- Add sugar in ¼ tbsp at a time, stirring and tasting every 2-4 minutes to taste. Sugar should cut the acid but not over-sweeten the sauce. When you've reached the almost desired acidity, add in bay leaves.

- Reduce heat to a simmer, cover, and let steep, stirring frequently for 10 minutes.

PIZZA SAUCE

FROM CHAPTER 4 DAPHNE: THE CLOUD WAITED FOR HIM

PAIRS WITH MARGARITA PIZZA RECIPE

Ingredients

6 oz can of Contadina tomato paste

15 oz can of Contadina tomato sauce

1 tsp white granulated sugar to cut through the acid

2 tbsp fresh oregano

2 tbsp Italian seasoning

½ tsp garlic powder

½ tbsp garlic salt

3 Bay leaves

¼ tsp freshly ground black pepper

Instructions

- Add tomato paste and tomato sauce to a large saucepan and warm on medium heat, stirring frequently. Add sugar ½ tsp at a time every 2-3 minutes, tasting to ensure it isn't too sweet but that the acid is cut.
- When the acidity is just about perfect, add 3 Bay leaves, oregano, Italian seasoning, garlic powder, salt, and pepper.
- Cook over medium heat, stirring frequently for 5-10 minutes. Adjust seasoning to taste.
- If not used right away, store it in a large jar.

PESTO SAUCE

FROM CHAPTER 20 ODOHERTY: THE GHOST SHE SAW BESIDE ME

PAIRS WITH CHICKEN PESTO RECIPE

Ingredients

2 cups packed Basil

⅓ cup pine nuts or walnuts

2 large Garlic cloves

⅔ cup Olive oil

½ a Lemon

Salt and pepper to taste

½ cup Parmesan or Polly-O Pecorino Romano

Instructions:

- Wash basil. Pat dry.
- Add nuts and garlic to the food processor and pulse until finely chopped (10 seconds or so).
- Add basil, salt and pepper, and a squeeze of lemon and process again until it resembles a paste (1 minute).
- While it is still running, drizzle olive oil.
- Add parmesan and blend for 1 minute more.
- If storing, drizzle a small amount of olive oil over the top to seal it in. Store in a jar and refrigerate.

HOLLANDAISE SAUCE

FROM CHAPTER 10 O'DOHERTY: THE SEASON OF GIFTING

PAIRS WITH EGGS BENNY RECIPE

Ingredients

3 egg yolks

1 ½ tablespoons fresh lemon juice

4 tbsp melted unsalted butter (cooled)

¾ cup unsalted butter (melted)

½ tsp salt

Dash Cayenne pepper

Instructions

- In a pot, heat either pre-made sauce or place egg yolk in a saucepan and whisk until lemon yellow and slightly thick, about 1 minute.
- Add 2 tbsp cold butter to the egg picture, then place the pan over very low heat, whisking constantly while the butter melts. Continue whisking until the mixture is thick enough to see the bottom of the pan when slowly scraping the bottom.
- Remove the pan pot from heat. Whisk in remaining cold butter, 1 tbsp at a time, until mixture is constant.
- Whisk in melted butter a little bit at a time. Season with salt, pepper, and a dash of Cayenne pepper.

CAESAR DRESSING
FROM CHAPTER 23 DAPHNE: CATCH A SHOOTING STAR?

PAIR WITH STEAK AND CAESAR SALAD RECIPE

Ingredients

4 garlic cloves minced or pressed

2/3 cup olive oil

1 1/2 muddled/juiced lemon (discard peel and seeds and strain out the pulp) about 1/3 cup juice.

2/3 cup grated Parmesan or Polly-O Pecorino Romano

1/8 cup (1oz) Worcestershire sauce

1/2 tsp salt (pink Himalayan preferred)

½ tsp freshly ground black pepper

Instruction

- Mince garlic gloves or press and put them in a bowl. Add the rest of the ingredients.
- Mix thoroughly. Store in a sealed container.

—BREAKFAST

- Eggs Benedict
- Cloud 9 Eggs and Toast with Bacon
- Pancakes Fabians Way
- Acorn Squash Eggs and Bacon
- EXCERPT FROM CHAPTER 20: The Ghost She Saw Beside Me with bonus commentary from the author

EGGS BENEDICT

FROM CHAPTER 10 ODOHERTY: THE SEASON OF GIFTING

PAIRS WITH HOLLANDAISE SAUCE RECIPE AND BISCUITS RECIPE

Ingredients

2 eggs

2 tbsp unsalted butter

2 slices of Canadian bacon

2 Slices of Swiss cheese

1 tomato, sliced

1 avocado, sliced

Premade Hollandaise Sauce OR see the recipe

Pillsbury flaky biscuits OR see the recipe

Instructions

- Bake biscuits according to directions OR see biscuit recipe.

- Slice tomatoes and slice avocado into slivers and set aside.

- Melt butter in a non-stick skillet over medium heat.

- Crack in eggs, keeping them separate, and when egg whites are nearly set, add hot tap water to the pan, enough to cover the bottom of the exposed pan.

- Cover and cook until the steam has cooked the layer of egg whites that is over the yolk, or longer if you like your yok cooked more. (About 30) and season with salt and pepper. Lower the heat and lay one slice of Swiss cheese on each egg. Cover until the cheese is sagging and melted over the egg. Remove from heat.

- Meanwhile, heat 1 tbsp butter on a frying pan over medium-low heat, and fry Canadian bacon until lightly browned.
- Heat Hollandaise sauce OR see Hollandaise sauce recipe.
- Cut biscuits in half and fill with egg, tomato, avocado, and canadian bacon. Top with biscuit.
- Spoon Hollandaise sauce over the biscuit.

CLOUD 9 EGGS AND TOAST WITH BACON

FROM CHAPTER 18 DAPHNE: DEFINITELY TABOO

Ingredients

4 slices artisan bread toasted (see recipe for Artisan Bread)

4 large brown eggs

1 Hass avocado, sliced

Nonstick cooking spray

4 slices of thin bacon

2 tbsp unsalted butter softened

Pinch pepper

Pinch of pink Himalayan salt

Instructions

- Preheat the oven to 350 degrees. Line a baking sheet with parchment and coat with nonstick cooking spray.
- Let the butter rest at room temperature.
- Separate the egg yolks from the egg white, putting the egg whites into a medium bowl and the yolks into another bowl. Reserve egg shells to scoop the yolks out individually later, OR use an empty water bottle to suck the yolks up.
- Add a large pinch of salt to the egg whites and beat with an electric mixer on low speed until stiff peaks form, 2-3 minutes.
- Divide the egg white puffs into 4 rounded balls on the baking sheet. Make a small well in the middle of each with the back of a large spoon.
- Bake the egg whites on the top rack until they are firm, no longer wet, and just beginning to turn golden brown, about 6-7 minutes.

- Meanwhile, place bacon on a skillet over medium heat. Fry bacon until crispy. Set aside on a plate lined with paper towels to soak up extra oil.
- Toast artisan loaf until lightly brown. Spread with softened butter. Lay sliced avocado on the toast— season with salt and pepper to taste.
- Gently transfer 1 yolk into the well of each egg white cloud. Bake until the edges of the yolk just start to set while being runny 3-4 minutes, or longer if desired. Salt with Pink Himalayan salt and freshly ground pepper as desired.
- Carefully transfer 2 egg white clouds to a plate. Serve with artisan toast and bacon.

PANCAKES FABIANS WAY

FROM CHAPTER 14 O'DOHERTY – MY SAFE PLACE

Ingredients

1 ½ cup white flour

4 tsp baking powder

1 tsp pink Himalayan salt

1.5 tsp coconut sugar

1 tsp vanilla extract

2 tsp anise extract OR 2 tsp ground anise seed

1 ½ cup whole milk

3 tbsp unsalted butter melted

1 egg

Coconut oil

Instructions

- Mix dry ingredients in a large bowl using a sifter to work the flour into a fine powder.
- Create a well in the middle of the dry mix.
- In a separate bowl, beat the egg for 2 minutes with an electric mixer on medium OR for 5 minutes by hand. Gently mix wet ingredients into the egg mixture.
- Add wet mixture to dry mixture and stir. Don't fuss over lumps, but work them out if you can.
- Preheat the skillet to medium-low (a drop of water should sizzle and evaporate right away).
- Melt 1 tsp coconut oil in a skillet. Pour about ¼ cup of batter at a time into the pan.

- When bubbles form over the surface of the pancakes, flip them with a flat-edge spatula. Wait twice the time it took for the bubbles to form before removing them from the skillet.
- Spread a thin slice of butter over the tops of the pancakes and cover with foil until the batch is done.
- Serve with real maple syrup.

ACORN SQUASH EGG AND BACON

FROM CHAPTER 27 O'DOHERTY: CRYING AT HER FEET

Ingredients

1 acorn squash

1 tbsp Red pepper flakes

Pink Himalayan salt to taste

2 tbsp Fresh thyme

3-4 eggs

3 tbsp Olive oil

6 slices of thin-cut bacon

Instructions

- Preheat the oven to 350 degrees. Spray a baking sheet with cooking spray.
- Cut an inch off of either end of the squash. Cut the remaining squash into ½ inch rings, trying to create a smooth, even surface. Scoop out the seeds and membrane from the center.
- Brush olive oil on both sides of the squash and place on a foil-lined baking sheet. Sprinkle it with salt and red pepper sparingly.
- Bake for 15 minutes or until tender.
- Crack an egg in each center and sprinkle it with the remaining salt.
- Bake at 350 degrees for 12 minutes more or until eggs are cooked to your liking.
- Meanwhile, add 4 pieces of bacon to a skillet in an arch shape, and 2 pieces arranged however. Fry in a skillet over medium heat until bacon is

crispy. Set aside on a plate lined with a paper towel to soak up excess oils.

- When squash and eggs are done, plate two acorn squash side by side with a single arch of bacon in a happy face arrangement.
- Use the remaining unarched bacon to crumble on top of the acorn squash.
- Garnish with fresh thyme leaves.

EXCERPT FROM CHAPTER 20 O'DOHERTY: THE GHOST SHE SAW BESIDE ME

WITH BONUS COMMENTARY FROM THE AUTHOR

The hospice nurse was just outside of Mrs. Soto's room, charting at a pod desk on her computer. She was a tall, blond woman with a pink stripe of hair on the bottom layer that curled out through the side. I approached her carefully, not wanting to startle her the way Lyndie had startled me.

"Hi there. I'm O'doherty. Ms. Soto was on a medication trial that I'm coordinating. I hear she decided to stop taking it."

"Oh hi!" The nurse responded, full of life and calm happiness. I thought it oddly fitting, although ironic, given her specialty. "I'm Penny, her hospice nurse. And yes, sweety, she signed on with hospice this morning. We're arranging to get her home and comfortable. I was told she started refusing all medications a few days ago, though if that helps."

"Yes. Thank you. It does." I took a note down. "And…her nurse told me she's hallucinating?"

"Well, it might seem that way but no, not really. You see, many times when a patient is close to death, they experience a phenomenon called deathbed visions. It has many nicknames, but essentially, dying people will often see a loved one who has long since passed away. They have conversations with them and everything. Mrs. Soto is currently visiting with her deceased sister, Mable."

"That sounds… terrifying," I said with wide eyes.

"No, on the contrary, the visits usually bring the patient a lot of comfort and joy and help them feel at peace with their death," she responded cheerfully. "Usually they'll tell them they're 'going on a trip,' and it's not long after that."

"And are there any coordinating factors in patients who experience this, clinically or otherwise?" I asked, strictly for documentation purposes.

"None. People from countless religions, ethnicities, cultural backgrounds, and ages have all experienced the same thing. No injuries, no weird lab results. It just happens."

"Do you mind if I see her? I have to enter an assessment."

"Oh sure, sweety! I'll be right here. You just let me know if you need anything!"

When I walked into the room, Mrs. Soto was indeed sitting up in bed, eyes wide and looking at an empty chair, laughing authentically and talking to no one. She had an energy you wouldn't expect from a dying patient. This was one phenomenon in hospice patients that I *did* know about. It causes the patient to have a "last kick" of energy right before they pass. A "rally," as they called it, often tricked family members into thinking their loved one was making a sudden recovery when, in actuality, it meant the exact opposite.

"Mrs. Soto, I'm sorry to interrupt."

"Oh hi, dear. I was just talking to my sister. We haven't talked in years!"

I made my way to the seat and decided to pull up a new one so I didn't sit on her dead sister. I looked uncomfortably at the empty chair next to me but smiled at Mrs. Soto to feign acknowledgment of her invisible visitor.

"Mrs. Soto, I won't be long; I just have to ask you some questions, if that's okay."

"Sure, dear. Mable doesn't mind. She doesn't have anywhere to be. She's dead!" She laughed but goosebumps pricked my skin.

"Oh. Okay… How are you sleeping? Any more sleepwalking?"

"No, no. No sleepwalking. I'm sleeping *fine*. The dreams are pretty wacky, though!" She laughed.

"Dreams? Tell me more about that."

"Oh, there's a handsome man—a broody sort, though. He just floats in the sky making storms," she said nonchalantly. The goosebumps came back. "Oh, Mable, that's not very nice."

"How long have you dreamt about him?" I asked typing the familiar data into her chart.

"Since the night of the storm. You know the tornado that took the old folks' home?" I clacked at my computer keys as she spoke, entering in her exact quotes. "Mable! No, no. That will scare the poor girl."

I smiled a small wince at the ghost and continued my questions at Mrs. Soto. "Why didn't you tell me about these dreams before? I've seen you several times since then."

"Oh, the medications made me fuzzy. I couldn't remember much of anything, much less a dream. You know how they disappear as soon as you open your eyes. Well, not so much now… N-Now, Mable, you just wait… Anyway! Since I've stopped taking the medications, I don't forget my dreams at all! And I *know* I've had them before. I wouldn't forget a man like *that*! Haha. Shirtless too! Ah! Now, Mable, *please*!"

"Wh…what would Mable like to share?" I offered, trying to rid her of the distraction. I gave a sideways glance at the ghost she saw beside me.

"Ugh, honey, she says you're being followed by a man. He doesn't like you looking into those rocks, and that if you don't stop, you might get hurt."

I felt the color drained from my face. Chills covered my body. I slapped my computer shut.

"See, Mable, the poor thing is spooked."

"Mrs. Soto, can you ask Mable what this man looked like?"

Mrs. Soto looked at the chair for a moment and then bucked her head in humor.

"Well, isn't that the darndest, that sounds an awful lot like the man in my dreams!"

"Mrs. Soto?"

"Yes, yes. He's a kind of light-brown-skinned man like Dr. Kumar. But has dark lips and white hair. Ahhh… Young man, though—about your age. *Handsome*, very handsome!"

My heart stopped for a long moment and I could feel my hands shaking. She described the man who was following me in exact detail. "Thank you so much. I'm afraid I have to go." I got up and started for the door.

"He's killed a lot of people, you know?" Her words made me freeze in place. "You should stop with the rocks, Mable says, or you'll be going on a trip like us soon!" Mrs. Soto turned back to the ghost and continued her conversation.

COMMENTARY FROM THE AUTHOR

Although this scene is pretty spooky, a few things about it are very special. The people and phenomena are not just there for theatrics. They aren't even there because I have a wild imagination.

The hospice nurse in this scene is inspired by two real hospice nurses, the real Nurse Penny and Nurse Hadley. Both are friends of mine from TikTok and educate their audiences on Hospice care. I strongly recommend Nurse Hadley's book, The In-Between: Unforgettable Encounters During Life's Final Moments, to anyone facing death. I am also looking forward to Nurse Penny's book, which, on the day of this publication, is not out yet.

You'll learn from these two extraordinary women that the phenomenon that Ms. Soto is experiencing in this scene is real! Death bed visions are precisely how the hospice nurse in this scene describes them. Now, I have not heard accounts of the "visitors" directly warning third parties of events like Ms. Soto is, but I have heard of them interfering with our world in some way to look after people they care about.

As a nurse, I have always been concerned about the general community's lack of understanding of what nursing entails. This is especially true of the work conditions portrayed in this book. Many of those complaints and conditions come from either my direct experience or complaints I've heard from other nurses while helping organize nurse unions. Through this book, I aimed to educate the reader about many of these things while taking them on an adventure.

—LUNCH

- Extra Stout Chilli
- Shrimp Toast
- Tuna Sandwich
- BONUS SCENE
- Zuppa Toscana
- Not Your Breakroom Pizza
- Stuffed Paprika Clams

EXTRA STOUT IRISH CHILI
FROM CHAPTER 28 DAPHNE: MY BROKEN WINDOW

Ingredients

1 1/2 lbs lean ground beef

1 large yellow onion, diced

8 garlic cloves, minced

5" fresh ginger root, peeled and minced

1 24oz can Contadina tomato sauce

1 29oz (or large) can black beans

1-1 ½ bottles Guinness extra stout

2 tbsp sugar to cut the acid

1 ½ tbsp McCormick chili powder

½ tbsp cinnamon

Salt and pepper to taste

2 cinnamon sticks

3-4 Guajillo chilies (depending on the desired spiciness) *They are usually found in a bag in the ethnic food section of your grocer.

Instructions

- Wash and prepare produce. Drizzle olive oil in a large pot over medium heat and brown 1 ½ lbs of ground beef, chopping it up and seasoning it with salt and pepper.

- Once browned, add diced onion & garlic clove, & ginger cook until aromatic (1-2min).

- Stir in tomato sauce, drained black beans, and ½-1 bottle of Guinness.

- Stir in sugar, chili powder, cinnamon, chili powder, salt, and pepper.

- Add 1-4 Guajillo chilis.

- Bring to a boil. Reduce heat to a low simmer. Cook for 15 minutes or until the broth is thickened, stirring frequently and scraping the bottom.

SHRIMP TOAST
FROM CHAPTER 1 - DAPHNE: IT'S A FULL MOON

Ingredients

12 fresh uncooked large shrimp

1 egg

2 ½ tbsp cornstarch

¼ tsp salt

Pinch of pepper

3 slices bread (premade or see Artisan Loaf recipe)

1 hard-cooked egg yolk

1 slice cooked ham (about 1oz)

1 green onion

1 cup vegetable oil

Instructions

- Remove the shells from the shrimp, leaving the tail and removing the vein. Cut down the back of the shrimp. Press gently open to flatten.
- Beat an egg, cornstarch, salt, and pepper with a fork until blended. Toss shrimp in the mixture until well coated.
- Cut the crust off of the bread and cut the bread into quarters. Place one shrimp, cut side down on each piece of bread, and press to adhere to the bread. Brush a small amount of egg mixture on each shrimp.
- Cut egg yoke and ham into ½ inch pieces.
- Chop onion.
- Place one piece of egg yoke, 1 piece of ham, and scant (¼ tsp) chopped onion on each shrimp.
- Heat oil in a wok to 37 degrees. Fry 3-4 pieces at a time in hot oil until golden brown (1-2 minutes).
- Drain on absorbent paper. This recipe will make 1 dozen.

TUNA SANDWICH
FROM CHAPTER 8 DAPHNE: A CLOUD RIDING CREEPER

Ingredients

8 slices of bread

2 tbsp butter

3 slices Swiss cheese

3 sheet of Romaine lettuce

6 slices of tomato

2 cans tuna in water

½ cup mayonnaise

¼ cup relish

2 stalks of celery chopped

½ shallots or 1 medium red onion

½ tsp pepper

½ tbsp celery salt

Instructions

- Drain tuna and put it into a medium bowl.

- Mix in mayonnaise, relish, celery, and onion. Then, salt and pepper to taste.

- In a skillet (preferably cast iron), melt 1 tbsp of butter. Toast 2 slices of bread on butter over medium heat until golden brown. When melted, add more butter to the skillet and flip the bread, browning the other sides.

- Reduce heat. Spoon tuna about 1 inch thick onto one slice of bread and reserve the rest of the tuna for another sandwich. Add Swiss cheese on the other. Cover until tuna is warm and cheese is melted.

- Remove from heat. Add Lettuce and tomato on top of tuna. Sprinkle it with salt and pepper. Top with bread that has Swiss cheese.

- Cut diagonally and enjoy.

BONUS SCENE
POL- CHAPTER 13

My body was battered from taking down the tornado. Luckily, Daphne patched me up well. She was an amazing healer. I would tell my sister about it. Ever since I found Daphne, Cynti has been asking about her incessantly. She would be unbearable tomorrow, considering I wasn't going home tonight. I needed to rest before I tried to fly home on a cloud.

My mother asked just as many questions as Cynti but with less enthusiasm. She was displeased that I didn't promptly drag Daphne home to the sky kingdom of Loanan against her will.

"Mother, this needs to be handled delicately. I've waited my entire life for-"

"This isn't about you, Pol. You know just as well as I do what the prophecies say. She needs to be brought in before anything happens to her."

"She is safe," I countered. "And has quite a lot of fight in her. She's not helpless."

"She's been poisoned. How do you reconcile that with safety?"

"Mother, give me time. She will come of her own free will and train. I give you my word."

"You have one moon cycle."

"Two."

"Don't push it!"

"We had a rough start. I'll make it right with her first. Besides, as soon as she disappears from her Realm, Ouran will know we've found her and strike."

Mother pondered for a moment, sipping her wine. She rose from the table, her long silver hair swinging around her front. "Make it right. Get her to settle her affairs. And then bring her home, Pol. War is coming whether Ouran knows we've found her or not. You're playing a dangerous game, son."

That night, I left for Miami in Regnum Solo. I sat under Daphne's tree and waited. The first week, she waved strangely with one finger and didn't come out. As disappointed as I was at her reluctance to engage, I was glad just to be near her. I finally had peace of mind that I could keep her safe. As the weeks went on, she came out to talk to me. I loved every second of being around her and learning about her, even if she was stubborn. I lived for moments when her abrasive façade broke, and she let her smile slip. But she wouldn't commit to coming with me to Loanan. It didn't bother me much at first. It was good to know she wasn't recklessly agreeable. But Mother was losing patience as Daphne kept her walls high.

Seeing her turn away from me night after night while the bond pulled me to her was not how I envisioned our meeting. She kept taking her poison, and it kept her comfortably unaware of how unbearable this felt; how my heart twisted, and how the zipper of my pants had to restrain me.

As unfortunate as it was for her parents to be in danger tonight, the opportunity finally won real trust with her. Even if it nearly killed me to fly off and rescue them from the storm, Daphne was riddled with guilty gratitude and a new understanding of my intentions. Since I had returned, barely able to stand on my own, bleeding and battered, she cared for me. She drew my bath and then promised to come to Loanan with me. I sank into the water as she washed and dressed my wounds, iced my welts, and offered me her spare room for the night.

The bed was soft and warm. My tired, naked body sank into it, and I covered my lower half with a plush comforter before she could return. When she came in with a hot soup, it was all I could do, not to sigh with relief. I added a healing elixir that would make my sleep deep and restorative.

She sat on the bed, to ensure she had enough to eat. I could have lost my patience, thrown her down, and taken her. Instead, I ate the hearty soup and let it warm my bones. I didn't want her to leave. So when she asked about the storm I saved her parents from, I went into great detail, all the way to the point that they slept through the entire episode. She laughed loudly. It put my heart in my stomach.

When she left the room, I closed my eyes quickly. Daphne was coming home with me in a matter of days. She would feel the bond soon, feel this incredible pull that I do. There would be no going back for her.

ZUPPA TOSCANA
FROM CHAPTER 15: DAPHNE: JUST ABOVE THE CLOUD LINE

Ingredients

2 boxes (8 cups) of Progresso Tuscany broth

2 cup water

1 lb ground Italian sausage (medium or hot)

1 medium yellow onion OR 2 shallots finely diced

1 stalk chives sliced (separating the whites from greens)

10 large cloves garlic (or 1 bulb) peeled and chopped into ¼-inch thick pieces

5 medium Idaho Russet Potatoes peeled and diced into ¼" thick pieces

3 tbsp celery Salt

1 tbsp Pepper

Two large organic leeks OR 3 small

1 bunch (about 6 cups) of kale deveined and chopped into bite-size pieces

1/4 cup half and half OR whipping cream

1 cup grated Pecorino Romano cheese

Instructions

- Wash and prepare produce. Separate the green leafy ends of the leaves from the hearty rings as you rinse them, as cooking times vary.

- In a large pot, brown sausage over medium heat, breaking it into chunks (about 5 minutes). Remove and set aside for later. Add diced onion or shallots and chive whites to the pot and sauté for 5 minutes until soft and golden. Add minced garlic to the same pot and sauté for 1 minute more.

- Add broth and water and bring to a boil. Add potatoes and cook for 15 minutes or until easily pierced with a fork. While boiling, add celery, salt, and pepper.

- With 12 minutes until the potatoes are done, add the green leafy ends of the leeks. With 10 minutes until the potatoes are done, add the heart ends of the leeks and cooked sausage. Let boil for 5 minutes, and then add the Kale. Bring to a boil again for 5 minutes.

- Add cream and boil for 1 minute more—season with more salt and pepper to taste.
- Add cheese just before serving.

NOT YOUR BREAKROOM PIZZA

FROM CHAPTER 4 DAPHNE: THE CLOUD WAITED FOR HIM

Ingredients

Premade pizza dough OR see the Pizza Dough recipe

½ tbsp Garlic powder

Premade pizza sauce OR see the Pizza Sauce recipe

16 oz shredded low-moisture mozzarella cheese

8oz package of BelGioioso Mozzarella Pearls

1 Roma tomato

2 large fresh oregano leaves, sliced into strips

1 garlic clove minced

4 large fresh basil leaves, sliced into strips

1 tsp ground black pepper

½ cup flour as needed to roll out dough on

Instructions

- Roll out pizza dough on a floured surface until ¼ inch thick. The pizza dough recipe will usually make a thick crust OR a thinner crust with leftover dough.

- Transfer the dough to the seasoned pizza pan. Brush the dough lightly with olive oil. Season the outer ring, or crust, with garlic salt as desired.

- Spread pizza sauce on the dough, leaving an inch or so border from the edge. Sprinkle oregano strips and minced garlic evenly over the sauced area. Then top with shredded mozzarella and tomatoes, leaving small spaces between them. Add mozzarella pearls as desired.

- Bake in the oven for 15-20 minutes at 400 degrees or until the crust is golden brown.

- Sprinkle strips of basil evenly over the cheesy area. Sprinkle lightly with freshly cracked black pepper. If desired, add shredded parmesan to the crust for a cheesy garlic bread crust. Bake for an additional 3-5 minutes.
- Let the pizza cool for 3-5 minutes. Cut into wedges and serve with a mixture of melted butter and garlic salt if desired.

STUFFED PAPRIKA CLAMS
FROM CHAPTER 12: O'DOHERTY: STAY AWAY

PAIRS WITH FARFALLE SALAD RECIPE

Ingredients

¼ lb crisp crumbled bacon (safe the fat)

2 tbsp olive oil

1 tsp Pepper to taste

1 tbsp Oregano to taste

2 tbsp minced onion or shallots

2 cups chopped clams (canned)

1 cup bread crumbs

12 medium clam shells OR 24 small

1 tsp Paprika

2 oz shredded mozzarella

Instructions

- Drizzle a 10-inch frying pan with 1 tbsp olive oil and heat over medium heat. Add bacon and cook to a crisp. Set bacon aside, crumble it, and save the fat in the pan.
- Add oregano and pepper, and let sizzle for a moment.
- Add onions and cook for about 5 minutes, stirring occasionally.
- Remove from heat and stir in bread crumbs and clams with clam juice.
- Fill clam shells with mixture. Sprinkle paprika on top and bake until done. In the last few minutes, you may sprinkle shredded mozzarella on top.
- Serve with farfalle salad (see recipe).

—SIDES

- Farfalle Salad
- Prociutto Wrapped Asparagus
- Braised Carrots
- BEHIND THE SCENES: Samanthas Carrots
- Mac & Cheese
- Twice Baked Potatoe

FARFALLE SALAD
FROM CHAPTER 12: O'DOHERTY: STAY AWAY

PAIRS WITH STUFFED PAPRIKA CLAMS RECIPE

Ingredients

12 oz box of Farfalle noodles

1 medium Red onion (diced)

4.23oz (½ 9.5oz jar) Kalamata olives (sliced)

1 Cucumber (sliced into 1" thick wedges)

9 oz Cherry tomatoes (halved)

1 large Organic Bell Pepper (diced)

7 oz Feta cheese crumbled

½ cup or hand full of Fresh parsley chopped

1 tbsp Celery Salt

½ tbsp Pepper

8 oz Greek dressing

Instructions

- Cook pasta until al dente. Rinse in cold water and set aside.

- Dice red onion and then soak in ice water for about 10 minutes.

- Meanwhile, wash and prep other produce.

- Combine noodles, olives, tomatoes, cucumbers, bell pepper, ¾ of the feta cheese, and parsley in a large bowl. Season with salt and pepper to taste and mix. When the onion is done soaking, add it to the bowl and mix thoroughly.

- Mix in Greek dressing to coat.

- Top with remaining feta cheese crumbles and refrigerate. Serve cold. Serves 8.

PROSCIUTTO WRAPPED ASPARAGUS
FROM CHAPTER 7 O'DOHERTY: DARLING RITUALS

PAIRS WITH REVERSE SEAR STEAK RECIPE AND MACARONI AND CHEESE RECIPE

Ingredients

1 lb of the thinnest sliced prosciutto the deli can do (a smidgen over shaved. The amount may vary depending on the size and amount of asparagus you get). Have the deli put paper between the thin slices; otherwise, it will rip when you try to separate them.

2 tbsp olive oil

3 Garlic cloves iced (OR to taste)

3 sprigs Rosemary fresh and chopped (OR to taste)

4 tbsp Pecorino Romano grated cheese (OR to taste)

Instructions:

- Preheat the oven to 325 degrees.

- Wash and trim asparagus.

- Line a baking sheet with parchment paper.

- Wrap each asparagus with prosciutto, starting at the tip and working down the shaft as far as possible. Lay the wrapped asparagus pieces on the parchment paper.

- Drizzle the asparagus with olive oil and sprinkle with garlic and rosemary to taste. Then lightly crust the asparagus with Pecorino Romano Grated cheese.

- Bake until asparagus is tender and prosciutto is slightly crispy (about 20-25 minutes).

BRAISED CARROTS
FROM CHAPTER 16: DAPHNE "CAN YOU FEEL IT?"

PAIRED WITH HERB ROASTED TURKEY RECIPE AND TWICE BAKED POTATOES RECIPE

Ingredients

3 pounds of carrots peeled and sliced into ½" diagonal pieces

½ cup Kerrygold unsalted butter (divided)

2 tbsp honey

2 tbsp brown sugar

½ tbsp cinnamon

1 ½ tsp salt

½ tsp freshly ground black pepper

Instructions

- Wash and peel carrots. Slice into ½" diagonal pieces.
- Heat a 12" skillet over medium-high heat. Melt 6 TBSP butter. Add carrots and stir to coat. Cover and cook for 15-20 minutes.
- Remove the cover and cook for 5-10 minutes more, stirring occasionally, until carrots are tender or easily pierced with a fork.
- Add the remaining 2 tbsp of butter, honey, brown sugar, cinnamon, salt, and black pepper. Increase heat to medium-high and cook for 2-5 minutes until the honey mixture is syrupy and thickened.
- Serve warm.

BEHIND THE SCENES: SAMANTHAS CARROTS

My sister, Samantha, can make anything taste good. I wouldn't say I like roasted carrots, but for some reason, when she makes them, they're so good. I originally had a recipe for braised carrots pulled from my late paternal grandmother's recipe collection, but truth be told, it was awful. When I tested that recipe, which called for orange juice and bitters, I couldn't stomach it and even got cramps. I immediately called my sister and said, "Sam, I need your carrots recipe. It's a bookish emergency." But like most of my family, she doesn't really have a written recipe for most of her dishes; She kind of just eyeballs it and knows. But she was able to help me come up with something. When I tested her carrot recipe, it still wasn't as good as when she made it, but it was pretty close. There's just something about eyeballing your ingredients that these strict measurements will never live up to.

MAC AND CHEESE
FROM CHAPTER 7 O'DOHERTY: DARLING RITUALS

PAIRS WITH REVERSE SEAR STEAK RECIPE, AND PROSCIUTTO WRAPPED ASPARAGUS RECIPE

Ingredients

¼ cup butter or margarine (melted)

¼ cup of flour

¼ tsp dry mustard

¼ tsp Worcestershire sauce

½ tsp salt

¼ tsp pepper

2 cups milk

2 cups shredded extra sharp cheese

2 cups cooked corkscrew macaroni

Instructions

- Preheat the oven to 350 degrees.

- Cook corkscrew macaroni until al dente. Drain and set aside.

- Meanwhile, over medium heat, blend butter, flour, mustard, Worcestershire sauce, salt, and pepper in a saucepan. Then slowly add 2 cups of milk. Mix until blended.

- Keep on medium heat until thickened, stirring occasionally. Add cooked corkscrew macaroni and mix together until coated.

- Transfer to a casserole dish and bake for ½ hour.

TWICE BAKED POTATO
FROM CHAPTER 16: DAPHNE - CAN YOU FEEL IT?

PAIRED WITH HERB ROASTED TURKEY RECIPE AND BRAISED CARROTS RECIPE

Ingredients

4 small red potatoes

15 oz Ranch Dip

1 cup thick shredded Cheddar plus extra for topping

Olive oil with truffle seasoning OR olive oil and truffle seasoning separately

Pink Himalayan salt to taste

Garlic powder to taste

Pepper to taste

Instructions

- Preheat 400 degrees on broil.

- Wash potatoes and poke holes in the skin with a fork. Microwave 4 ½ minutes per potato.

- Slice the potatoes down the middle about halfway through. Scoop out the insides, leaving just enough to keep the potato's shape. Reserve the insides in a medium bowl.

- Spray/brush potato skin with olive oil inside and out. If you don't have truffle olive oil, sprinkle truffle seasoning on after. Truffle salt can be very salty, so use it sparingly. Season with garlic powder. Season with salt if not using truffle salt. Season with pepper to taste.

- Use an air fryer or top rack of the oven to broil skin/shell until crispy but not burnt (5-10 minutes).

- Meanwhile, mash the potato insides in a medium bowl. Add ranch dip and continue to mix until moist and smooth.
- Mix in 1 cup of cheddar cheese until blended.
- Reduce heat in the oven to 350 degrees. Fill baked potato skins with mixture. Top with shredded cheese.
- Bake again for 5-9 minutes on the middle rack.

—SALADS

- Greek Salad at a Party
- Arugula & Mango Salad
- Steak & Ceasar Salad
- BEHIND THE SCENES: @ZachReadsBooks

GREEK SALAD AT A PARTY
FROM CHAPTER 40 O'DOHERTY: IF I SURVIVE HIM

Ingredients

5-6 grilled chicken tenderloins (or protein of your choice)

1 tbsp garlic salt

Pepper to taste

2 hearts of Romaine lettuce

4.23oz (½ 9.5oz jar) Kalamata olives

4-6 oz pepperoncini (as desired)

4 oz cherry tomatoes halved

½ red onion, sliced

2oz- 3oz Feta cheese (as desired)

Salt and pepper (to taste)

3 tbsp olive oil

3 tbsp balsamic vinaigrette.

Instructions

- Cube chicken tenderloins and season with garlic, salt, and pepper. Grill or pan roast in an air fryer until golden brown and at least 165 degrees internally (about 15-18 minutes).

- Meanwhile, rinse the lettuce thoroughly. Chop the romaine into bite-size chunks. Spin in a salad spinner or dry to prevent wilting. Transfer to a large bowl.

- Pile on olives, pepperoncini, tomatoes, red onions, and feta cheese to taste.

- Salt and pepper to taste.

- Tear the stem and top from a few pepperoncini and spill juice over the salad. Lightly drizzle oil and balsamic over the Greek salad.

ARUGULA & MANGO SALAD
FROM CHAPTER 32 DAPHNE: THAT ROCK!

PAIRS WITH CARIBBEAN JERK PULLED PORK RECIPE AND
COCONUT CRUSTED CROISSANT RECIPE

Ingredients

6 oz arugula

6 oz spinach

1 mango (preferably the cotton candy mangos if available

4oz bag of sliced almonds OR pine nuts(optional)

2 tbsp olive oil

2 tbsp balsamic vinaigrette.

½ tsp sriracha

Instructions

- Rinse the arugula and spinach. Put them in a salad spinner or dry them to prevent wilting. Transfer them to a large serving bowl.
- Skin and cube fresh mangos. Place it on a bed of arugula.
- Sprinkle in the nuts to taste.
- Mix olive oil, balsamic, and sriracha. Drizzle to taste.
- Salt and pepper to taste.

STEAK AND CAESAR SALAD

FROM CHAPTER 23 DAPHNE: CATCH A SHOOTING STAR!?

Ingredients

About 1.50lb Bottom Round Steaks thin sliced

2-3 fresh romaine hearts (OR just under 1 lb romaine lettuce)

1 cup garlic croutons (OR as desired)

½ cup Parmesan cheese (OR to taste)

4 oz cherry tomatoes halved (OR to taste)

Black truffle salt to taste (Use sparingly)

Freshly ground pepper to taste

Garlic powder to taste

Instructions

- Season steak with truffle salt, garlic powder, and pepper to taste. Truffle powder can be salty, so use it sparingly. Set aside, letting rest for 30 minutes.

- Trim the ends off of 2-3 romaine heart stalks. Cut the romaine into 4-5 chunks. Rinse the leaves, pulling them apart, taking care to remove any embedded dirt between them. Discard stiff yellow centers from the bottom chunk if desired. Put the lettuce in a spinner or dry to prevent wilting. Once dried, transfer to a large serving bowl.

- Heat olive oil over medium heat in a cast iron skillet. Cook steak, searing the outside. Cook each side for about 30 seconds per side, flipping twice, for a total of 2 minutes or less OR until it's reached the desired doneness. Keep an eye on the meat's edge to see the amount that is cooked through. Take care not to overcook as it is a thin slice. When cooked, set aside on a plate, stacking the pieces and allowing the juice to collect.

- When ready to serve, put in individual bowls. Dress each salad with premade dressing (or see Caesar dressing recipe), parmesan cheese, croutons, and tomatoes as desired. Mix well. Add ½ tsp of steak drippings to each salad and mix well again.
- Slice steak into strips and place the desired amount over individual salads.

BEHIND THE SCENES: @ZACHREADSBOOKS

While writing Opals and a Nimbus on my laptop one night, I scrolled through TikTok on my phone. A TikToker in the bookish niche I befriended, Zach, was on LIVE. I decided to write while listening to him talk. I came to a crossroads with my character at that time, not really sure what should happen next or how to propel the scene to where I wanted it to go. So I picked up my phone and jokingly asked Zach in the comment section what should happen to my character next. As it turns out, he chose defenestration! He didn't know at the time that the character had not come into her power enough to survive that or that she was thousands of miles above the ground/sea when this would happen. He also didn't know that I had a spicy scene plotted for this chapter. Now, questioning Zach was honestly supposed to be a joke, but I decided to challenge myself and write in a scene where Daphne gets pushed out of a window, at 12+ miles above the earth's surface, with not nearly enough magical ability to save herself, right before a spicy scene breaks out. It worked perfectly and ended up being one of my favorite scenes to write! Zach also decided earlier in the book that Daphne would "almost knock" on Pol's door but then "decide not to and walk away." This was a much easier decision for me to work in, but I want to acknowledge all of Zach's contributions all the same.

—DINNER

- Wild Boar Stuffed Green Pepper
- Chicken Pesto
- Reverse Sear Steak
- Manicotti
- BONUS SCENE
- Herb Roasted Turkey and Gravy
- Caribbean Jerk Pulled Pork
- BEHIND THE SCENES: The Jerk Sauce
- Beef or Pork Chow Mein
- BEHIND THE SCENES: Grandma Marian

WILD BOAR STUFFED GREEN PEPPERS

FROM CHAPTER 1 - DAPHNE: IT'S A FULL MOON

Ingredients

3 large green peppers

1/2 lb ground wild boar or ground beef

1 cup dried bread crumbs

1 tbsp chopped onions

1 tsp salt

¼ tsp pepper

1 can (8 oz) Contadina tomato sauce

Instructions

- Preheat the oven to 350 degrees.

- Clean the peppers and slice the top off near the stem like a pumpkin. Clean the seeds out as best you can.

- Bring 1 cup of water and ½ tsp salt to a boil. Add the peppers and cook them for 5 minutes. Remove the peppers with a slotted spoon, being careful not to rip them. Set them aside in an ungreased glass baking dish (about 8x8x2) and drain the water.

- Add 1 tbsp olive oil to the bottom of a pan over medium heat. Add meat and cook until done. Drain excess oil and transfer meat to a medium bowl. Mix the remaining ingredients in the bowl until well blended.

- Lightly stuff each pepper with ⅓ the meat mixture. Stand peppers upright in the baking dish.

- Cover with regular foil and bake for 45 minutes. Uncover and bake for an additional 15 minutes.

CHICKEN PESTO

CHAPTER 20 O'DOHERTY: THE GHOST SHE SAW BESIDE ME

PAIRS WITH PESTO SAUCE RECIPE

Ingredients

1 box spiral tricolor pasta

1 tbsp butter

1 lb chicken tenderloins

4 oz bag of pine nuts

3 oz bag sun-dried tomatoes julienne cut

9 oz bag of fresh spinach

8 oz package of fresh mozzarella pearls

8 oz container of pesto sauce OR see recipe

Salt to taste

Pepper to taste

Garlic powder to taste

Tarragon to taste

Instructions

- Bring a large pot of salted water to a boil. Add pasta and cook as instructed—strain and transfer to a large serving bowl.

- Cube chicken tenderloins. Season with salt, garlic powder, and pepper, and then tarragon. Bake until cooked through (350 degrees for 18-20 minutes or internal temperature is 165 degrees). Add to pasta.

- In a skillet, melt 1 tbsp of butter. Add Spinach and cook until moist, stirring frequently. When Spinach is soft but not overcooked, add it to pasta. Add sun-dried tomatoes, pine nuts, and pesto sauce (see pesto recipe) to the pasta. Mix. Add mozzarella pearls last and mix through.

REVERSE SEAR STEAK
FROM CHAPTER 7 O'DOHERTY: DARLING RITUALS

PAIRS WITH PROSCIUTTO WRAPPED ASPARAGUS RECIPE AND MACARONI AND CHEESE RECIPE

1 ½– Steaks in a 250°F oven			
Doneness	Time in oven (min)	Goal Temp in oven	Final Goal Temp
RARE	20-25	105°F (40°C)	120°F (49°C)
MEDIUM RARE	25-30	115°F (46°C)	130°F (54°C)
MEDIUM	30-35	125°F (52°C)	140°F (60°C)
MEDIUM WELL	35-40	135°F (57°C)	150°F (66°C)
WELL	40-45	145°F (63°C)	160°F (71°C)

Ingredients:

1 ½ thick cut beef steak (Filet Mignon preferred)

1 tbsp Pink Himalayan salt (OR to taste)

1 tbsp Freshly ground pepper (OR to taste)

1 tbsp Garlic powder (OR to taste)

1 tbsp Vegetable oil

2-4 tbsp Kerrygold unsalted butter divided

4 rosemary sprigs plucked

3 garlic cloves minced

Instructions

- Preheat the oven to 250 degrees.
- Take the meat out of the refrigerator. Season it evenly with salt, pepper, and garlic powder on both sides. Let it sit at room temperature for at least 30 minutes.

- Set steaks on a wire rack in a rimmed baking sheet lined with foil for easy clean-up. Cook steaks in the oven until the thermometer shows the goal in-oven-internal temperature for your desired doneness (see chart above). This can take 20-45 minutes; see the chart above for cooking time that correlates with desired doneness.

- 4 minutes before the steak comes out of the oven, heat a large pre-oiled cast iron skillet. Heat until smoking or searing hot (water should bead and steam quickly, OR olive oil should move quickly in the pan. Try with no more than 1 tsp of either, taking care not to get burned).

- Add 2 tbsp butter until melted. Quickly add minced garlic. Cook, stirring frequently, until fragrant, about 1 minute, taking care not to let the garlic burn. Quickly add rosemary. Don't worry about getting rosemary steps in the mixture; it adds a nice woody taste.

- Add steaks and the rest of the butter to the skillet and sear until each side is well browned, about 30 seconds each. Use tongs to hold steak(s) sideways to sear edges, taking care not to overcook past desired doneness. Check internal temperature with a meat thermometer, frequently comparing it to the chart above for the goal final internal temperature. As they cook, use a metal spoon to baste the steaks if desired.

- Reverse-sear steaks do not need to rest and will continue to cook for a short time after being removed from heat unless they are sliced. Serve right away.

MANICOTTI

FROM CHAPTER 14 O'DOHERTY: MY SAFE PLACE

PAIRS WITH MANICOTTI NOODLE RECIPE AND PASTA SAUCE RECIPE

Ingredients

4-5 cups Pasta Sauce (Pre-made OR see pasta sauce recipe)

1 box Manicotti noodles (Premade and cooked OR See manicotti noodle recipe)

Filling Ingredients

1 ½ lb Polli-o ricotta

6 oz Polli-o mozzarella cheese cubed

½ cup Polli-o grated romano

Salt and pepper to taste

1 tbsp chopped fresh basil chopped

12 oz bag of fresh spinach

Medium Italian sausage cooked, crumbled, and drained (if not using Pasta Sauce recipe)

Instructions

- Preheat the oven to 400 degrees.

- In a large bowl, mix all of the filling ingredients together.

- Lay manicotti noodles in a glass baking dish. Put 2 tbsp of filling in each manicotti rectangle and roll it up OR fill cooked premade noodles (sizes will vary, and filling amount will also). Press the edges together to prevent the filling from coming out.

- Line the noodles in the glass baking dish next to each other until you have a single row. Cover with pasta sauce and sprinkle with grated romano cheese.

- Bake uncovered for 30 minutes.

BONUS SCENE
POL- CHAPTER 16

Daphne was finally here. She came home to Loanan, my kingdom in the Realm of the Skys, hidden above Miami. She didn't like to fly on my nimbus cloud, but I hoped that watching the sunset above the cloud line made up for it. It always brought me a sense of serenity.

I watched the sun set behind Miami every day since I was sixteen. I flew out after my mother had explained bonding ceremonies. My mother, the queen, was not subtle about the conversation in any respect.

"Everything went as planned with the ceremony. They conceived your fated mate, a girl, and we conceived you. But then war broke out over a prophecy. Their kingdom fell, and the king and queen were presumed dead. We don't know where your mate is or if she is alive, son," my mother said.

"She is."

"How do you know?"

"I can feel it." I dug my training blade into the dining room table.

"Pol, remove your weapon from my dining table and put it away."

I pried it out, and a small 2" gash marred the wood. I went to stab the table again, but the weapon flew from my grip and into my mother's. Her power was the strongest in the kingdom, and she never let anyone forget it. I glanced at her sideways. "Are we done?"

"No. We need to secure allies, Pol. You will be courting Princess Briella in-"

"Briella? We hate each other. Absolutely not, mother. My mate *is* alive. I am not courting anyone. Especially not *Briella*."

"You couldn't possibly know that she is alive."

"But I do. Just like you knew when Dad died oceans away. You felt the bond break. My bond isn't broken." She stiffened. Our dinner came out: herb-roasted turkey and gravy with candied carrots and a twice-baked potato. She thought my favorite food would smooth this over.

"We need a backup plan. If she is alive, no one can find her. We've been looking for 16 years. No one expects you to marry tomorrow. Court Briella—"

I threw my food off the table, the plate shattering against the wall and the foot spattering across the floor. Mother yelled my name as I stormed out.

I had a nimbus formed before I was halfway down the hall. I was a better rider than my mother or anyone else. I flung the front doors open and flew out of the palace. Faster than she could make it to the doorway, I had ported out of Loanan and into the Regnum Solo, the Realm of soil where the humans lived.

The air was dirty and coarse, but the sunset was best here. This is where I could feel it the most; the bond was strongest in the Regnum Solo. Mother may not believe it, but I knew, looking down at the darkening human city, that she was down there somewhere unprotected.

I watched the sunset every night, wondering where she was and if she was safe and happy. I wondered if she was scared or resilient. I wondered what she looked like and if she knew about me. I'd never look at another girl, and I'd sabotaged every courting attempt by my mother—all for a person I didn't know. I'd kill for her. My eyes turned to opals within weeks.

Now, in that same dining room, my opal eyes focused on my mate, who was enjoying my favorite dish just as much as I did. I poured her a glass of Rhubarb wine that I had imported from a restaurant in her Realm. "Welcome home, Daphne," I said, raising a toast. She didn't say anything, only gave me a sly smile that choked my heart. I'm sure she wanted to deny this was home, but she would never be able to escape me.

She *was* safe. She *was* happy. She *was* strong and, fearless and bold. And she was incredibly beautiful. I couldn't have imagined a more perfect person. Sure, she was rough around the edges and headstrong, but she was also smart and careful, great qualities for a future queen. I watched her at this moment, and she seemed so happy. Fear hugged my throat.

I didn't know how she would respond to what I had to tell her, what I had kept from her, but the time had come. We had finished our wine.

"Walk with me."

HERB ROASTED TURKEY AND GRAVY

FROM CHAPTER 16: DAPHNE "CAN YOU FEEL IT"

PAIRS WITH TWICE-BAKED POTATO RECIPE AND BRAISED CARROTS RECIPE

Ingredients

1 package (4-5lb) Boneless, skinless turkey or chicken thighs

1 cup cooking vinegar to rinse chicken

2 tbsp Garlic powder (OR to taste)

2 tsp Pink Himalayan sea salt (OR to taste)

2 tsp Freshly ground black pepper (OR to taste)

3 tbsp Tarragon (OR to taste)

Gravy Ingredients:

1 ¼ cups of low sodium turkey/chicken broth divided.

¼ cup white flour sifted

1 TBSP Better Than Bouillon chicken flavor OR 1 large cube of Knorr Chicken Bouillon

¼ cup Holland House cooking sherry

Instructions

- Preheat the oven to 325 degrees.

- Rinse the turkey in vinegar and let it drip dry.

- Place turkey thighs in a small, shallow baking dish lined with foil. If the dish is much wider or longer than the amount of meat in it, roll the foil toward the thighs, leaving a few-inch border.

- Sprinkle garlic powder on the turkey to coat it in a thin crust. Next, salt and pepper the thighs. Then, sprinkle tarragon liberally on top. Don't worry about getting seasoning in the bottom of the pan; it will season the drippings.
- Bake at 325 degrees for 25 minutes or until it reaches an internal temperature of 165 degrees.
- In the last 8 minutes or so, heat 1 cup of broth to a boil in a large pan. Reduce heat to a simmer. Stir in Better Than Bouillon and Cooking Sherry. Let it simmer for 4 minutes.
- Meanwhile, in a small Tupperware container or jar, add ¼ cup of cold broth and ¼ cup of sifted flour. Secure the lid and shake until thoroughly mixed.
- When the turkey is done, set the thighs aside on a dish and cover with foil, reserving the drippings. Add the turkey drippings from the foiled baking dish to the pan of simmering broth, along with any seasoning that was left on the pan.
- Slowly whisk the flour and broth mixture, a quarter cup at a time, into the simmering broth mixture, breaking up any chunks. Gravy will thicken as it cools, so stop adding cooled broth and flour mixture before the gravy gets too thick on the stove.
- Slice turkey and serve with a drizzle of gravy on top.
- It pairs well with Coopers Hawk Rhubarb wine.

CARIBBEAN JERK
PULLED PORK
FROM CHAPTER 32 DAPHNE: THAT ROCK!

PAIRS WITH ARUGULA SALAD RECIPE AND COCONUT
CRUSTED CROISSANTS RECIPE

Ingredients
Marinade
6 sweet peppers diced

1 red onion diced

2 bunches of green onions (scallions) sliced

1" ginger, peeled and minced

3-6 habaneros diced (depending on your preferred spice level)

½ cup allspice

1 TBSP Thyme

¾ tsp nutmeg

¾ tsp cinnamon

1 TBSP pepper

1 TBSP salt

2 TBSP garlic

1 TBSP crushed red pepper

¼ cup dark brown sugar

¼ cup low-sodium soy sauce

¼ cup canola oil (or coconut oil)

¾ cup Apple cider vinegar

½ cup orange juice (I prefer with pulp)

1 lime

Other Ingredients
1 3/4 lb pork loin

Instructions

- Prep produce. Reserve cores and trimmed pieces to make a broth with later if desired.
- In a medium bowl, add sweet peppers, red onion, scallions, ginger, and enough habaneros to reach the desired spice level. Three habaneros will be medium spice, and six will be very spicy. Mix together.
- Add allspice thyme, nutmeg, cinnamon, pepper, salt, garlic, crushed red pepper, and dark brown sugar to the first bowl and mix until coated and brown.
- In a separate bowl, mix in soy sauce, oil, apple cider vinegar, and orange juice. Squeeze in 1 lime.
- Slowly stir the wet mixture into the first, mixing thoroughly. Add to a crock pot with pork loin and marinate refrigerated overnight.
- Cook in a covered crock pot for 5-6 hours on low or 3-4 hours on high, ensuring pork is cooked through.
- Take the pork out and set it on a cutting board. Shred the pork with two forks. Add it back to the crock pot with the marinade.
- Use a slotted spoon to scoop it out and let it drain before serving it on the plate. Serve with Arugula Salad and Coconut-Crusted Croissants (See recipes).

BEHIND THE SCENES: THE JERK SAUCE

This Caribbean Jerk Pulled Pork recipe is near and dear to my heart. When I was in nursing school, I lived in a tiny apartment. To deal with the stress of nursing school, I decided to perfect my recipe for Caribbean Jerk sauce. I started by buying all the different Caribbean jerk sauces at the local grocery store and tasting which one I liked most. Then, I compared the ingredients on the back. I bought every ingredient and then a few extras that I thought would bring the flavor out better. I made this Jerk Sauce five times before finding the correct measurements for each ingredient. When I make it, I have to tone down the peppers, as my husband is a bit sensitive to the heat. The dish has evolved a lot in its presentation. I knew immediately that the arugula salad with freshly cut mangos would be an amazing side. The croissant with coconut was once a shell for the meat to be stuffed inside, like a giant cannoli, but it would get too soggy, so I decided to make them traditional rolled croissants brushed with egg wash and pressed with coconut flakes. This is, to this day, my favorite dish I've ever come up with. It will be second only to the Shrimp and Grits recipe that I will eventually perfect!

BEEF OR PORK CHOW MEIN
FROM CHAPTER 33 O'DOHERTY: TELL ME YOU UNDERSTAND

Ingredients

Chow mein noodles

10 stalks of celery

3lb yellow onions

2-10 oz or bigger sirloin, skirt or flank steak, thin cut or pork.

Garlic powder to taste

Freshly ground black pepper to taste

Soy sauce

1 tbsp white granulated sugar

2 cans bean sprouts OR 8 oz fresh

1 tbsp cornstarch

¼ cup oil

Instructions

- Cook low mein noodles according to the package instructions. Drain and rinse under cold water to prevent the noodles from sticking together. Set aside.
- Meanwhile, wash and trim celery. Slice at an angle into 1" thick pieces. Wash, peel, and trim onions. Chop onions into half-arch strips.
- Slice steak or pork into thin strips and season with garlic powder and pepper.
- In a large wok, heat oil over medium heat. Add meat and cook until browned. Remove from the wok and set aside.
- In the same wok, add celery and cook until it is soft. Add onions, 1 cup water, bean sprouts, sugar, and soy sauce.

- Cook for 20 minutes. Then add 1 cup water and cornstarch. Stir. Add noodles and meat and toss in a hot wok until coated and warm.
- Top with sesame seeds.

BEHIND THE SCENES: GRANDMA MARIAN

My late paternal grandmother hand-wrote this recipe, and while I will admit it is not the best I have ever had, it is special to me because it is hers. The scene where this dish makes an appearance actually featured yet another pizza. This would have been the third time pizza appeared in the book. So I decided to let Grandma determine what the characters were eating, and I stuck my hand in the pink folder of recipes she left behind and pulled out beef or pork chow mein.

—DESSERTS

- Apple Pie
- Tam & Pecan Pie
- Frozen Chocolate Al'Orange Cheesecake
- BONUS SCENE
- Watergate Salad

APPLE PIE
FROM CHAPTER 7 O'DOHERTY: DARLING RITUALS

Ingredients

Filling:

1 pie crust

1 large egg yolk, slightly beaten

5 ½ cups fresh, peeled, sliced Granny Smith

1 tbsp lemon juice (omit lemon juice if apples are tart)

½ cup granulated sugar

¼ cup firmly packed light brown sugar

3 tbsp all-purpose flour

¼ tsp salt

½ tsp ground cinnamon

¼ tsp nutmeg

Topping:

¾ cup all-purpose flour

¼ cup sugar

¼ cup light brown sugar, firmly packed.

⅓ cup butter or margarine at room temperature

Instructions

- Preheat the oven to 375 degrees.

- Beat the yolk from 1 large egg in a small bowl. Brush the bottom and sides of the pie crust evenly with the yolk. Bake on a baking sheet until light brown, about 5 minutes. Remove the crust from the oven.

- Wash, core, peel, and slice apples. A spiral cutter will work best for this. Combine sliced apples, lemon juice, ½ cup sugar, ¼ cup brown sugar, 3

TBSP flour, ¼ salt, ½ tsp cinnamon and ¼ tsp nutmeg into a medium bowl. Mix well and spoon into the prepared pie crust.

- Mix the remaining flour, sugar, brown sugar, and butter in a bowl with a fork until crumbly. Sprinkle the topping mixture evenly over the apple mixture until covered.
- Bake on a baking sheet until the topping is gold and the filling is bubbling; about 50 minutes. Cool on a wire rack (at least 1 hour). Serve warm with vanilla ice cream if desired.

YAM AND PECAN PIE
FROM CHAPTER 30 O'DOHERTY: OH. MY. GOD.

Ingredients

Filling

2 18 packs PicSweet yam patties or ripple sliced yams

½ cup packed light brown sugar

1 tbsp pumpkin pie spice

½ tsp salt

1 cup whole milk

3 whole organic eggs, beaten

Topping:

⅓ cup softened margarine or Kerrygold unsalted butter

¾ cup packed light brown sugar

1 cup finely chopped pecans

Crust:

One 9 inch deep-dish frozen pie crust.

Instructions

- Thaw the yam patties or ripple-sliced yams and mash them into a paste. Then, combine the filling ingredients in the same bowl. Fill the pie crust.
- Combine the finely chopped pecans, sugar, and margarine in a separate bowl. Sprinkle evenly over the top of the pie filling.
- Bake 350 degrees in the oven for 30-40 minutes or until the crust is golden brown.

FROZEN CHOCOLATE AL'ORANGE CHEESECAKE
FROM CHAPTER 3 O'DOHERTY: LIKE A LABYRINTH

Ingredients

8 oz package of softened cream cheese

1 ounce can of sweetened condensed milk

1 cup melted and cooled semi-sweet chocolate

½ cup undiluted evaporated milk

5-ounce thawed, frozen orange juice concentrate

1 Kebler ready prepared pie crust shell

Orange peel

Instructions

- Take frozen orange juice out to thaw. If not using a premade pie shell, prepare the shell.
- Beat cream cheese smooth in a small mixer bowl. Slowly add sweetened condensed milk.
- Melt chocolate in a small pot and then add in the chocolate. Mix until blended.
- Add in the evaporated milk; blend until smooth. Add orange juice concentrate; blend for one minute.
- Pour into the pie shell. Freeze for 1 ½ to 2 hours.
- If you have leftover filling, try making cake bars in an ice tray or silicone mold.
- Slice 2 large curls of orange peel and use as garnish.

BONUS SCENE
FABIAN- CHAPTER 14

I tried not to show my nervousness as I put together the quick dessert for the BBQ. It wasn't too hard to hide; Dotey was taking an extra long time fixing up her hair before we left. She always looked beautiful, even when it was a frizzy mess. I dressed in jeans and a nice blue polo. I put a little extra cologne on and some hair puddy in my curly hair to make it look neat. Luckily, the dessert I was whipping up wouldn't get me too messy.

I plopped the entire Cool Whip container in the bowl with the pistachio pudding and pineapple. I smiled, remembering the first time Nana made this for me.

"Your grandfather and I stayed in the Watergate Hotel on the night of June 16th, 1972. We dined in their restaurant and decided to try the little green pudding they were bringing around. Your grandpa had three servings!" Nana had told me as she put the walnuts in a baggy and hammered them with the flat side of a meat tenderizer. That night, the president of the United States got caught in a scandal at that very hotel! The pudding was famous after that."

"Can we use the colorful marshmallows, Nana?" I had begged her.

"Yeah! The pink and green ones!" Melly called, jumping up and down.

Nana winked at us and pulled a colorful bag of tiny marshmallows from the cabinet. "You mean *these?*"

We cheered and hopped around. The dessert was done in no time, but when Melly and I saw it, we glanced sidelong at each other.

"I don't know Nana. This looks like… bad," Melly had said.

"Hmmmm. Then I guess you'll never know if it is. Oh well. More for me and gramps!"

We exchanged looks, trying to decide if we wanted to try it.

"Okay, one extra cherry, though," Melly said.

The first scoop was so cold and delicious. Our eyes went wide with delight.

"What did I tell you?" Nana had said victoriously. "It's something else.

We ate two bowls and would have had a third if Nana hadn't cut us off. Melly demanded it for every birthday and Thanksgiving. It never got old.

Now a grown man, I made it for the millionth time still remembering that day vividly. I knew it may not be received well today at first glance. No one ever wants to try it at first, but once they do, it becomes an instant favorite. I finished stirring and folding the ingredients until thoroughly blended and then carefully spooned them into a fancy glass dessert bowl. As I placed it in the freezer to chill, my phone buzzed behind me.

"Hello?"

"Hi, is this Fabian Levy?"

"Yup, this is he," I said, sucking some spare whip cream off of my finger.

"Hi, this is Dorris from Downey Jewelers. We certified the yellow diamond you brought in. It's stunning, by the way. We've never seen anything so pure."

"Thank you. My mother left one for my sister and me. She found them with my dad after he passed."

"Oh, how nice. Well, it is ready to be mounted. Do you have a ring size and style in mind?"

"Well…"

"Honey, are you almost ready to go?" Dotey called from the other room.

"Yup, all set when you are, Honey," I hollard back. I whispered into the phone. "I don't, but I'm gonna get the size in the next couple weeks and fish through her jewelry box for ideas on the style. Can I come in two weeks?"

"Sounds great, hows-"

"Sweety, is this dress okay?" Dotey asked.

"I'll call you back soon, Mike. I gotta go!" I said and then disconnected the call. Dotey was twirling in a beautiful white sundress with pink flowers on it. The fabric looked like it was micro-quilted and scooped low at the neck. "You look beautiful, Honey."

"You always say that."

"You always look beautiful," I said, pulling the Watergate salad out of the freezer. "Ready?"

She rocked on her tiptoes to look at the strange green pudding as I topped it with crushed walnuts and a few maraschino cherries. "Whaaat's *that*?"

"Watergate salad. Try it." I handed her a small spoon. She took it and only hesitated a moment before scooping it up. I could tell she was preparing to fake like she liked it, especially since her face morphed to surprise when she finally tried it.

"Oh, wow! That's really good."

I smiled and gave her a kiss. "You ready?"

She sighed and nodded. I put the glass lid on the dish, and we headed out to meet her godmother.

WATERGATE SALAD
FROM CHAPTER 14 O'DOHERTY: MY SAFE PLACE

Ingredients

1 package (3.4oz box) of instant pistachio pudding mix

8 oz frozen whipped topping (thawed)

1- 1 ½ cup miniature marshmallows

1 (8oz) can of crushed pineapple with juice

⅓ cup (4oz) chopped pecans or walnuts

Maraschino cherries (garnish)

Instructions

- In a large bowl, combine pistachio mix, crushed pineapple with juice, mini marshmallows, crushed nuts, and Cool Whip topping.
- Mix thoroughly with a plastic mixing spoon.
- Chill for 1-2 hours before serving.
- Serve in a fancy glass dessert bowl.
- Garnish with walnuts or pecans and maraschino cherries.

Authors Favorite Recipe

CHECK OUT THE NOVEL

Opals & a Nimbus: Book I
Paperback: ISBN: 979-8-9887358-2-3
Hardback: ISBN: 979-8-9887358-0-9
Ebook: ISBN: 979-8-9887358-1-6

Acknowledgments

Acknowledgments First and foremost, I want to thank my husband, David. You've been my number one beta eater and my constant cheerleader. Thank you, Mom, for allowing me to use your recipes. Thank you to Aunt Ella and Cousin Donna for helping me decipher Grandma's recipes. Thank you to my sister Samantha for saving my butt when the braised carrot recipe from grandma's stash turned out to be disgusting, and you helped me fix it. Thank you to everyone who tried the food and read the book. I hope you enjoy it!

ABOUT THE AUTHOR
NANDER

Born and raised in Florida, NANDER has worked as an ICU nurse, activist, social media influencer, and union organizer. In early 2023, she reconnected with her passion for reading and writing as a means to cope, finding a new favorite genre of spicy romance. Wanting to spread her imaginative wings and share her passions for teaching, empowering, and storytelling, NANDER put her knowledge and creativity to paper. Now a mother, wife, and author, NANDER brings her genre-hopping, rule-bending preferences to the table in original written works.

facebook.com/NurseNander

twitter.com/NanderNurse

instagram.com/NurseNander

tiktok.com/@NANDER